THE SEARCH FOR THE
SHADOW CAT

THE SEARCH FOR THE
SHADOW CAT

BOOK 3 *of the* JAGUAR ORACLE SERIES

KURT MÄHLER

ILLUMIFY
MEDIA.COM

www.kurtmahler.com

The views and opinions expressed in this book are those of the author and do not necessarily reflect the official policy or position of Illumify Media Global.

Published by
Illumify Media Global
www.IllumifyMedia.com
"Let's bring your book to life!"

Library of Congress Control Number: 2025911921

Paperback ISBN: 978-1-964251-59-2

Cover design by Debbie Lewis
Map by Cody Oakley

Printed in the United States of America

For my daughter Sarah
You were born, the war withdrew, and peace returned.

ORION

BEAR CLAW
RANCH

DIAMONDBACK
RANCH

PINE LINE FARMS

OLD CENOTE

OLD BARN

EL
PEQUEÑO
JARDIN

RANCH HAND
TRAILER PARK

DUNES

LAGUNA
MADRE

EDEN'S BEND

AIRSTRIP

PALM VALLEY

LAGUNA
ATASCOSA

EDEN'S
BEND

TRIPP'S OBSERVATION
LODGE

0 mi   5 mi

CROSS LAKE

WASH
OF
CHOCO

SAN BENITO

INDIAN
LAKE

LA PALOMA

EL PALACIO

ENCANTADA-RANCHITO

SALAZAR'S
WOOD

BIRDING
CENTER

PALO ALTO
BATTLEFIELD

SAN PEDRO

MEXICO

TEX

N
W   E
S

LOS COMPADRES

ESPERANZA
FARM

DEAN PORTER
PARK

PALO VERDE
ESTATES

RESACA DE
LA PALMA

BROWNSVILLE

PALO PALOMA
WILDLIFE REF

0 mi   5 mi

URSA MAJOR
& MINOR

MATAMOROS

UNIVERSITY

SANTA ROSALIA
CEMETERY

CAMPESTRE
DEL RIO

VILA PANC

SABAL PALM
SANCTUARY

CUMA
OF

EJIDO

GREEN ISLAND
(COLONY OF THE LOST)

LAGUNA
MADRE

EL REALITO

SOUTH PADRE
ISLAND

VIRGO

- RIVER/RESACA
- ROADS
- COASTLINE
- TREES/FOREST AREA
- MARSH
- RANCH BORDER
- EDEN'S BEND

SWOG'S
WALLOW

LAGUNA
VISTA

GASTON
RANCH

EN'S
ND

PORT ISABEL

GULF OF
MEXICO

LAUNCH PAD

BAHIA
GRANDE

SOUTH BAY

AS

BOCA
CHICA

PALMITO
HILL

LA BURRITA

THE LADY RIVER (RIO GANDE)

RIVER'S
END

EL
CONCHELA

SOUTHMOST

GORGAS
OASIS

EL RANCHITO
Y REFUGIO

ORENO

LA ESPERANZA

OPHIUCHUS

CONTENTS

I want to find the country whence the shadows fall.

—George MacDonald
The Golden Key

1

ALWAYS BEGIN

If turmeric can draw the pain
And onion of care purge you
Then add some ginger, cat's claw too
While dandelions urge you:

"Now rest and heal, now breathe and know
That time is never wasted
When blended with the seasonings
Our lives have thus far tasted."

Like slender eucalyptus blades
That hang down for the taking
Converting strength to grace when we
Release them in their breaking

Green leaves containing secret oils
That give life in their losing
The leaves of time turn daily green
We pluck them by our choosing

Thus were the meditations of the lord of the Valley in the barn of Brazos Ben. The bees remembered them, hearing the words as they brought their sweet treasures to a hive behind the barn's bone-dry rain-collection gutter. They passed on the meditations to the flowers of the prairie pleatleaf and the lemon beebalm, a memory they stewarded from then on, season to season and bloom to bloom.

Each evening Oracle would reflect in a quiet song. Each morning he would recall one thing to contemplate until it became a wonder. Sometimes it was a day from his youth. Sometimes it was a night on his journey that began with the discovery of the fallen monarch butterfly in his Yucatán home of Sian Ka'an. Other times it was a recollection of a day before his own days had begun, the Days of First Things, when creation was fresh, and the animals knew their names, and Eden breathed innocent air uninterrupted by invisible jealousies. Yes, from whichever of these realms of recollection it was, Oracle would choose one memory. He would consider it again, experience it again, discover in it a new thing he had not yet realized until commonplaces became epiphanies.

And in this way, the cat of the Long Journey was not "doing time" as one in a hospital bed or a prison cell would describe it. No, he was *redeeming* time, such that by the time Oracle was able to stand on his legs and walk without limping in the stall of Brazos Ben's barn, he was not a heavier cat, but he was a *weightier* one.

From Christmas through the Blue Moon of spring, the lord of the Valley healed while the night sky displayed its dramas. On the zodiac of that turning dome, Virgo, the virgin queen, sojourned, a harvest-promise of wheat in her left hand, a palm frond of praise in her right. In turn, she gave way to Libra, the great scales of justice, to whom the planet Jupiter gave honor as he passed. Then the fairness of Libra ceded space to the threats of Scorpio, the scorpion. Sagittarius, the centaur, strung his bow as he rose, ready to pierce that devil through the heart, attacking at dawn each late-April morning. The planet Mars looked over his shoulder, assessing his skill at striking the mark.

But before Sagittarius could prance proudly on the celestial stage, a strange starry host rose to prevent his victory, a rogue who was alien to the zodiac, a Man known as Ophiuchus—the Serpent Bearer—a constellation where a Man and a boa constrictor wrestled. Each night the two contestants passed above Oracle before they sank behind the trees, the Man ever tying the serpent into a knot, and the serpent ever loosening the knot again as it uncoiled the arabesques of its body.

Oracle pondered the wrestling match in the heavens. "Alas, oh Man. Wherever you forbid the snake most to move, that becomes the very leverage point from which the rest of the beast coils all the tighter around you."

Night after night, the match transpired above the jaguar, the Man ever trying a new wrestling hold on the serpent, the foe ever discovering, from that very place of earnest pressure, a new constricting power.

The moon observed the struggle in the final nights of May, moving with the rolling pair like a referee. Her full-moon attention now spent upon the contest, she entered the first night of June and looked upon the Cat Who Remembers, who kept watch through the barn's broad windows. Oracle saw her.

"Oh moon, a boa like this seeks the manchild named Miracle too. One who, like this serpent among the stars, seeks a spot to slither through and devour the lad. May the Maker and the Namer protect him."

And the moon listened with a luminous compassion reaching far across the land in response to that prayer, even as far as the window where the boy slept in the frail cabin of his foster parents. Her moonbeam kissed the child's cheek like a mother adoring her slumbering son.

"Yes," the moon said, "may it be so. And until we see how the story of Miracle unfolds, I will keep watch with you.

For you have taken up the prayer of Kahoo, the last jaguar of seventy springs ago. You have put your paw forward."

"Thank you, oh Lamp of the Night. I have done what was in my heart to do, and oh, how costly it has been! I am content with the choices I have made, and their cost, but I do not know how the prayer of Kahoo will be fulfilled."

"Nor do I, oh Seeker of the Lonely Tree, but this I know. You are of the Flock of the Lion. You are a descendant of those animals who gathered on the isle in the Gihon River the day Eden closed its gates, a day so full of woe I hid my face for seven nights behind clouds and shadow. And during those nights, it was the knowledge of what I had seen on Gihon Isle that gave me hope. Yes, the sight of a tribe of animals so varied from one another, yet gathered as one, became a lamp in the night to me. And I knew that somehow the Maker's prophecy of how all would be made right again was already at work in coming true for Man and every living thing. This gave me courage to shine upon the face of the earth again."

The moon bid the jaguar farewell as she departed from view beyond the windows where Oracle watched. In her place glowed a deep and starlit sky.

"Her words have turned my longings into birth pains. We shall see how much time must pass before birth pains deliver joy."

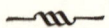

On the morning of the summer solstice, while the trees were still silhouettes beneath a pale-pink sky, Brazos Ben came to the jaguar.

"I've doctored you as best I can. The vet tells me you're about as good to go as I'll ever get you. Those two stubborn spots on your underside will clear up soon. But you'll have to bear the mark of that wound to your thigh like a Purple Heart medal. I can't do cosmetic surgery to smooth out that scar messin' up your coat. You'll have a story to tell your friends."

Brazos Ben knelt down to look at him through the bars of the stall.

Oracle considered the Man. The beard was thick, the hair heavy, and the red color of both fading fast beneath his equally faded hat.

But glimmering out from his eyes, just barely perceived behind the heaviness, is his soul. It stands like a lone mountain climber in distant alpine snows, looking at me in wonder.

Oracle came to the stall bars.

"You're as at ease with me as a friend sitting in a chair. I stopped drawing my Bowie knife within a week of your stay. Even after your strength came back, there was no need. Besides, a friend doesn't draw his knife on a friend."

Brazos Ben took a deep breath, lifting and dropping his shoulders as he did.

"I feel like a fella who's crossed a log over a creek and then watched the log drop away. Can't go back now that I'm here. It's time I do somethin' with you, partner. You're a jungle predator and not a barn owl. But honestly, friend, it's a tough hitch to untie. If I cut you loose right here in these parts, you won't last long. You'll be lucky if you make it out of the county alive. But I can't keep you here either. You weren't meant for stalls and straw. There's my son and all, but…"

The Man looked down at the straw beneath the jungle cat's feet.

He sighed. "Yeah, there's my son, but he's a busy man who's burned his bridges. I've burned mine too. Words like the ones we spewed at each other don't fade like steam, they scar like fire…makes a man retreat…makes a man build a stockade and lock the gate."

Oracle saw a cloud overshadow the Man.

He is no longer present. To be sure, his body remains kneeling at the stall gate before my face, but the Man's spirit, like his soul, has retreated to that snowy summit deep within him, a place where memories are stored.

The jaguar drew closer, his nose and whiskers just outside the bars. The Man, lost in a terminal memory, did not register the nearness, but continued looking upon the straw and the stubble.

Oracle breathed.

Deep within Ben, in a place where his nickname Brazos became silent out of honor for the depth, he found himself in another world. And in that world, Ben was a lone alpine traveler upon a snow-crowned ridge among peaks. The ridge was clear of clouds, the sky a crystal blue. Ben could see mountain ranges beyond his own, and here and there, far below, a hint of green vales and forests.

I could go down if I wanted to. I have more in common with trees than icy peaks. A man can live and abide and bear fruit like a tree, but he can't live long where the air's too thin.

A motion caught his attention. On the ridge and in the distance, a snow leopard sat upright, methodically curling his tail as he looked at Ben. The bank of snow around the cat reflected the sun, and its whiteness pierced Ben's eyes. He lowered his brim and turned around.

A woman stood on the summit with him just a few yards away. Her dark hair poured over her shoulders. She wore a long-sleeve, grooved turtleneck and a houndstooth-pattern skirt to just above the knees. Dark hose covered her legs, as did fashionable leather boots from a time gone by.

"You can let me go now, Ben," she said.

Beside her stood a child. Ben looked at him while the sun passed overhead.

Still the age of six, I see. Still wearing that yellow shirt, plaid paints, and red high-tops he was wearing that day he went to the hospital for chemo. That day I finally went with the doctors' decision. Luke lingered long, but he didn't return.

The boy smiled at Ben. "You can let me go too."

He reached for his mother's hand but remained looking at his father with a face placid and bright.

Ain't no pain there. No sickness. No sorrow. Only an innocence that gives off a warning. It's too much to look at for long.

Ben returned his eyes to those of his wife. She spoke.

"There is our older son, so why do you remain here? You've been in the Land of In-Between for fifteen years. Is that not long enough to soften the blows you gave each other before you ascended here and poured an avalanche on your trail? Is that not long enough for the snows to melt?"

"I can't forget what he said when you died," Ben answered. "He said I made you lose heart. He said I didn't do all I could to save you. 'First you let my little brother die by dragging your feet with the doctors; then you let Mom waste away while you drifted in darkness.' I can't forget the words he spoke to me."

"I'm not telling you to forget, Ben. I'm telling you to live. Tripp was a hurt kid makin' angry vows. He didn't know how else to stop the pain. He pushed you away, and that's hard, but don't let that stop you from living."

"I do live, honey. I've made my own Eden. Tripp's made his too, running hard in the opposite direction. My Eden is to hide among the trees, and his Eden is to hide among his trophies. We both have found a way to live."

"Yes, but alone. And it's not good to be alone. There's no peace in that. Like the mussels of the river bottom that you care for, you retain each grain of pain. But when will the grains become pearls, Ben? Even the mussels know how to redeem their pain. How about you? When will 'never again' become 'begin again'? You can always begin, Ben."

The boy leaned into his mom and smiled even brighter than before.

That light comin' off his face sure comforts and hurts at the same time. He looks just as happy as he was on that last birthday of his when he blew out all six candles and laughed until we had to calm him down for cake.

The boy opened his mouth wide, and as he did, the mountain, the woman, the child, and the sky disappeared into a radiant cloud. The child's laughter rang out, then he spoke.

"Always begin!"

The sound of a truck pulling up before the barn caused the vision to lift. Ben blinked. He found himself still kneeling at the stall bars. The jaguar's eyes, beryl green and steady, were before his own. He leaned forward until his face touched the cat's whiskers.

"You know what happened, don't you," he whispered.

The jaguar looked deep into him.

Tears came to Ben's eyes.

The truck horn sounded. A man spoke in a reedy tone with a thick Texan accent.

"Hey, Ben, I know it's early, but I brought you some company."

Brazos Ben cleared his throat, stood, and came to the front of the barn, closing its broad sliding door behind him as he stepped out. In the truck was a man in work clothes, his combed hair lying in the same well-oiled pattern it had lain in since high school. His rolled-up sleeves revealed arms that had seen the sun for many a day. With him was a woman the same age. She did not look toward Ben. She did not seem to be looking at anything at all. Her face was joyful, but her eyes were blank. She held a long white cane in her right hand.

"Jewel! Old friend!" said Brazos Ben. "I thought you lived in Tyler."

"I do, but I was passing through on my way to Waco to see my nieces at Baylor in their summer term, and I thought I'd see Art. We were talking, and I asked, 'Now where's that character Brazos Ben, the one who always had the loudest muffler in Falls County?'"

Brazos Ben laughed. "Well, I'm older and wiser than I was in those days, but I haven't gotten over workin' on cars!"

Art whistled at the wonder of the hermit's home, a three-story tree house in a massive southern live oak with running water, electricity, and every amenity an engineer like Brazos Ben could give it. "You haven't gotten over building new things either! Boy, Ben, you've outdone yourself! Jewel and I heard about this place down at the diner this mornin'. Folks there told us you don't like visitors, but I knew you wouldn't mind, especially since we've already downed breakfast. Golly, your place is more impressive in real life than they made it out to be."

"Come with me, and I'll give you a tour."

And the three retired to the tree house.

2

NIGHT RUN

The friends of the bottomland hermit stayed half the day. Oracle could hear them talking. Brazos Ben bid them farewell as Art chauffeured Jewel to Waco. For a long time, the host stood in the driveway looking in the direction his guests had departed, as long as it took the cicada to complete a cycle of her songs.

In the afternoon, Brazos Ben made a fig poultice for Oracle, placing it on two stubborn spots on the jaguar's skin still sore from the fight with the cougar. He offered the jaguar fresh water mixed with a small amount of herbs, and he set before him eggs, fish, and venison. Oracle considered him as he walked away.

The Man works in silence today. His thoughts are speaking to him.

Evening fell. Oracle kept watch at the windows. The stars of Leo the lion and his little brother gamboled over the barn. So did Ursa the bear and her cub. Venus sped past the lions on an errand of her own while two hunting dogs, unsure whether to chase lions or bears or speedy messengers, strained at the leash of their distracted master, a herdsman named Boötes, whose eyes had found the Crown of the North, Corona Borealis.

But beyond the crown and the canines glimmered the forty faint stars of the hair of Berenice, the queen who sacrificed her flowing locks to divine love in hopes of the safe return of her husband the king from far-off battles. And the king did return, not only to pick up where he had left off, but to decree a new calendar and a new era.

He began again.

The metal door of the barn slid open on well-greased rails. Brazos Ben appeared at the stall, carrying the same silence he had borne in the day. After a time, he took out his phone, pressed it, and lifted it to his ear when the ringtone sounded. A voicemail recording spoke.

"This is Tripp Menefee of InfoTech Menefee. From ranches to rockets, we've got the know-how you need. So glad you called. Leave your name and number, and my personal assistant Edwin will get back to you. Or text me a message and he'll do the same. Thanks!" The voicemail gave its signal to speak.

"Give me a call when you can, Tripp."

It was the eve of the seventh day after Jewel's visit. The air was still. Inside the barn, all slept. In the pen next to Oracle's, the flock of goats reclined, calmly dozing or meditatively chewing the cud. And though Brazos Ben did not know that in the time of the May new moon the goats had come to remember their names, he noticed they imparted the same peace as the cat and did not mind the feline's presence. And so he permitted them to abide as neighbors. Their peace produced a lingering calm, oiling the Man's work with his tools and mellowing the Man's wine at his table.

Oracle awoke to the sound of Brazos Ben's truck backing up to the barn. The door slid open. Brazos Ben stood there with Art, who held a pole with a catch-rope at one end.

"Here he is," said Brazos Ben. "You won't meet a calmer cat than this one. Prefers fresh fish to venison and wild hog."

Art whistled precisely the same tune of surprise he had whistled when he had seen the tree house. "Amazing! Who'da thunk a jaguar woulda come this far north! I've never heard of such a thing, not even in the tall tales of the Texas Rangers!"

Brazos Ben gave a self-satisfied grin. "Well, he's from the Waco zoo upriver, actually. He's been keeping me company for quite a while, and it's time for him to move on. But he won't last long here on his own, that's for sure. It's why I've asked you to come. We're takin' him somewhere, Art. Somewhere he's got a heck of a better chance than all the rifles in these parts give him. We're headed to the airstrip over by McClanahan."

"The airstrip! Ben, where you flyin' him?"

"I'll tell you when we get there. For now, let's just get him in the crate and on our way. We're supposed to be there at eleven, and it's a twenty-minute drive."

Art bent into an athletic stance, catch-pole at the ready. "Let's roll, then. Man, this'll be a story for the diner in the mornin'. They won't believe me. They'll think I had too much hooch out here. But then I'll show 'em pictures on my phone and watch their dentures drop out of their jaws. It'll be the talk of the town."

Brazos Ben grasped the catch-pole and stared hard at Art. "Keep my name and my place off your tongue. I want nothin' of it, and I don't want anyone coming here asking me to repeat what they've heard you gab about. It's why I didn't bring you out here the other day with Jewel. I knew a line of folks would show up, and I didn't move out here to draw a crowd. I don't want anyone saying, 'Art sent me to get it straight from the horse's mouth.' And if anyone asks you, 'Hey, didn't Ben nab that critter who escaped from the Waco zoo? The one that left paw marks up near Shaw Creek where it flows into the Brazos?' Then it's on your head to blow smoke. I don't want you dropping my name into any jaguar rumor. If they talk about that cat being on my land, you tell them about the cougar, ya hear? You got pictures of him that I sent you, and so does the vet. He's in cahoots with this shell game too. Show 'em the dead cougar photos like the vet's doing. Whatever yarn you spin, just don't connect my land with the jaguar. Do you understand, my big-mouthed friend?"

Art's face fell with a mix of disappointment and comprehension. "Yessir, I do. I'll bluff when I boast if that's your druthers."

Brazos Ben and Art rolled an aluminum crate up to the stall gate. Oracle stood, his tail signaling both curiosity and readiness. The two beheld him.

"Good golly, this cat looks like he owns the place," Art said.

"Oh, I'm sure he would if I let him. Even the goats don't mind his company. I moved 'em back into the barn when I saw how he calmed the goats down—Don't ask me how he did it. All I know is that the coyotes are a threat and the scent of this cat puts more fear into them than any sheepdog."

Art leaned on the catch-pole while he scratched his head, his well-oiled cowlicks begging for a comb as he did. "Ben, I got an idea. They already call you 'Brazos Ben' 'cause of your love for wildlife and the river. You could set yourself up sweet-like if you made somethin' of this rare find to the general public. You could make it work for you, ya know what I mean? People would pay to come here and take a look-see."

Brazos Ben frowned at Art in silence.

Art shifted uncomfortably as a wordless moment passed. He sighed as he spoke. "But I know you don't think that way, Ben. I know you prefer to be a stranger to folks and a friend to the river. Didn't used to be that way, but things happened and, well, I understand. Family stuff hurts somethin' awful and don't heal right quick. Hospital stays end and their bills get paid, but other debts are a long time in collecting. I know it's hard, friend. I'm sorry."

Brazos Ben breathed long through his nostrils. "Yeah, money debts are easy to pay off with a little patience. Other debts ain't so easy, just like you say. But I think you might be encouraged by what we're about to do. I'm gonna try to cancel a debt or two on the long list of IOUs tonight, Art. You'll see. But I can't speak for the other party, if he'll bury any hatchets or no. We'll just have to try and see. Let's get our guest into the crate."

Oracle understood. And even while Art readied his catch-pole, the cat came to the stall gate. Brazos Ben grinned, opened the gate, and watched with pleasure Art's astonishment as the jaguar willingly walked into the crate.

The Beechcraft King Air taxied to within a few yards of Art and Brazos Ben as they stood on the side of the runway. The props slowed as the plane powered down. The Falls County hamlet of McClanahan was asleep, as was the aging water treatment plant nearby. The airstrip itself was little more than a few hangars and a small building, a structure whose windows were a mosaic of glass and plywood. Two silent witnesses kept watch on either side of the strip, a green-and-white rotating beacon and a tattered windsock. A row of stinkgrass and cheatgrass grew in the seam where the strip met the parking tarmac. The moon was absent, for clouds were passing through the night sky, preventing her view.

The side of the King Air opened, dislodging from within as a rectangle swinging up from the fuselage. It rose to reveal two men, one slender with cabin-crew clothing and a narrow tie, the other with unkempt hair and a fitted shirt showing beneath a leather jacket. The crewman deployed a small set of stairs to the tarmac and descended first while the other delayed stepping down when he saw Brazos Ben.

Art tipped a nonexistent hat toward the man in leather and reached out his hand to the crewman. "Artemus McCracken. Glad to know ya. Welcome to the mighty metropolis of Marlin, Texas, former mecca of mineral baths and Major League Baseball. For spring training, that is."

"Edwin Connors. A pleasure to meet you. That was quite an introduction." Edwin looked around, eyebrows raised. "I see the airport lives up to Marlin's impressive reputation."

"Yeah, we've slumped a bit since our glory days." He offered Tripp a hand, for he now stood near.

"Artemus McCracken."

"Travis Menefee."

Brazos Ben remained motionless beside Art, hands at his side, looking at Tripp.

Edwin noticed and turned to the hermit of the Brazos with a slight bow.

"Edwin Connors at your service—Tripp's executive assistant."

"Ben Menefee."

Edwin nodded toward Tripp, but he remained stone still. Edwin abruptly offered Ben a handshake. "A pleasure to meet you, sir, and a pleasure to collaborate with you on this evening's unique opportunity. Mr. Menefee, you have provided us with remarkable assistance in the procurement of this virtually irreplaceable asset. I commend you for your creativity in apprehending him."

Brazos Ben shook his head slightly. "I didn't quite apprehend him. I just couldn't stand by and watch a good fella go down. Reminded me too much of somethin' I saw when I was small. So, I stepped in and backed him up. Just doin' the right thing, that's all."

"Well, your ethics are impeccable, I would say, including your commitment to confidentiality. Tripp informs me there will be no need to sign a memorandum of understanding on this matter."

"Nope. Not necessary. I'm in full agreement with the need to not make noise about your operation. Suits me fine."

Art, phone raised, took pictures right and left. Edwin looked distressed.

"And your companion, Mr. Menefee? Should we have *him* sign an MOU? Those photos he is taking are the intellectual property of InfoTech Menefee—um, your good surname notwithstanding...sir."

"Won't be necessary," replied Brazos Ben. "Art's an old friend. He won't do more with those photos than show 'em at The Cactus."

"Pardon me?" asked Edwin.

"It's a diner on the town square," said Brazos Ben. "The only folks there aren't the kind that use Facebook much. They work too hard to have time for that; only post when someone marries or buries."

Edwin registered his concern with Tripp, who nodded back calmly.

"It's okay, Eddie. I trust them. These are people of their word. When they say something, it sticks. That's good enough."

Tripp and Brazos Ben looked at each other with such absolute silence that the sound of the co-pilot and cockpit radio chatter reached them from within the plane. Edwin glanced at his watch, coughed, and put on a smile.

"Very well. Shall we continue with our joint operation?" He pulled out his phone, which cast a blue glow on his face. "The checklist shows that the next order of business is to make sure our stories are symmetrical. At Tripp's request, I have informed the zoo's public relations department that our lead on the location of the jaguar turned out to be a rogue cougar, possibly rabid, which Mr. Menefee had dispatched prior to our arrival. You will retain the evidence of the acquisition of that creature, Mr. Menefee?"

"Yep," replied Brazos Ben. "Better than that, if anyone comes looking, I'll point them to the trophy that CJ's Taxidermy made out of him. It's on display at the Gomez Feed Store."

"Oh, I see what's goin' on," Art said. "We tell the first layer of the story, but not *every* layer. Kinda like an onion. Grandpa used to say truth's a lot like an onion. If you go through enough layers, it always brings you to tears."

"Absolutely," Tripp said. "And we don't want to go there just now. No time for tears. We've got a development schedule to keep at Eden's Bend. It's why we shipped him off to the zoo in the first place. But it worked well that he escaped and disappeared. The schedule has space for him now."

The four Men maneuvered the crate to the cargo bay of the King Air. It was not until then, beneath the lighting inside the plane, that they were able to see the jaguar as more than an intimidating shadow. Each one bowed his head to set his eyes before one of the four small, barred portals that were the windows on the sides of the crate. Brazos Ben and Art were on one side and Tripp and Edwin on the other. They peered into the chamber. The ruddy-gold coat and rosette spots of the cat of the Yucatán shone like living heraldry through the portals, and the breathing of all slowed down.

The prince of Eden's Bend and the hermit of the Brazos lifted their faces from the windows at the same time and looked across the crate at one another, decentered by the beauty that disarmed them and appointed the moment. Tripp opened his mouth, a tear in his eye.

"Thanks, Dad."

"You're welcome, son."

3

WHAT THE MOON FOUND

The King Air roared away at 11:25 p.m. Art and Brazos Ben retired to the sitting room in the tree house, where they talked through the night over bottles of Shiner Bock.

"Our friend Jewel disturbs me," said Brazos Ben.

Art paused, the bottle partway to his mouth. "What do you mean?"

"I mean her blindness."

Art finished a swig. "But she's been blind since college. Why do you say it now?"

"Because she's so happy and believes in God," said Brazos Ben. He put down his empty bottle.

Art shrugged. "What's wrong with that? Is it wrong to be happy?"

"No, and it's not wrong to believe in God either. But to be both after going blind, that's troubling. How can she trust him when he didn't do a darn thing to prevent her from losin' her sight? If I were her, I'd take it out on him and go my way."

"You mean like a protest? 'God, I'm so mad at you that I'm not believin' in you anymore! No more church! No more money in the offering plate!' That kinda thing?"

"Well, I hadn't put it in those sorta words, but yeah, kinda pressing through on your own for contentment, since he didn't come through."

Art repeated the words as he idly looked at Brazos Ben's hunting trophies on the walls. "'Since he didn't come through.' Hmm. Now I'm no theology nut, but I wonder: Do you think it matters to him that you don't believe he's there?"

"What do you mean? How do I know? If he's there, I suppose he's too busy dealin' with wars and famines and such. I don't think he cares about these personal things we're going through. Not what I went through, at least."

"Oh, I see. So he's more of a big boss than a detail man."

"I suppose so."

Art put his empty bottle down and reached for another. As he opened it, he glanced out the window, where, in the light of the full moon, he saw the branches of the great oak their room rested among.

"But this tree we're sittin' in and these poles holdin' up your house: I'd say they carry a whole lot of details in your life, Ben, even though they ain't soundin' angel trumpets about it. Every floor of your dream home is anchored by 'em. The trunk of this here tree is the center of it all, like the hub of a Ferris wheel at the county fair, where it's the biggest thing without sayin' so much as a word, so big you'd have to be blind as a bat not to see it. Now, as for this big ole oak, I could say to it, 'I don't care for you, tree,' and it would still serve as the heart of the house, no thanks to me. I just wonder if it's the same with God. I wonder if he's at work more than we know; it's just that either we ain't noticing or ain't caring. Kinda the same things we're pointing a finger at God for not doing."

Brazos Ben reached for another. The bottlecap gave a long hiss as he slowly opened it. "Never thought of it that way, Art. Helps that you're a Baptist."

Art blushed. "Well, I'm a backslidden Baptist with this beer in my hand! But I don't think it's really 'drinkin',' ya know what I mean? It's more like 'takin' it easy.' It's the *hard* stuff that counts. Now, *that's* a red line."

Brazos Ben smirked. "Seems to me religion's all about exceptions. I think whoever cooked it up was the same one who engineered the IRS! They're all about what 'counts' and what doesn't too! Who can know every law and loophole, let alone do 'em?"

"Yeah, I don't got nothin' to crow about when it comes to knowin' much more than I've already told ya about the Maker. I know he's there, and I know he cares, and I know he's good. That's about as far as my brain can figure things out with all the sawdust cloggin' it up. Carpenters don't have much time to philosophize."

Brazos Ben swigged and nodded. "I understand what you're sayin,' Art, and I appreciate you shootin' straight with how you see Jewel's situation. Still, it troubles me 'cause it doesn't add up. It ain't *good* she went blind, and it ain't *right* for God to leave her that way. But Jewel herself doesn't live there. She lives in another world, as if she *can* see and as if he *is* good. I wouldn't believe it if I didn't know her myself. But she's more joyful now than she was in our tailgating days. Me, well, I'm worn out, but she has a strength; from where, I don't know."

Art swished the beer like mouthwash as he swallowed. "Yeah, Jewel's a gem—get it?"

Brazos Ben rolled his eyes. "You always do become a poet by the third bottle. Anyway, seeing her left me wondering… wondering if I need to ask my questions again. 'Cause I have to say that right before you and Jewel pulled up the other day, I was lookin' at that jaguar, and something I can't explain happened. Something very specific I can't talk about just now. But it stirred something in me. Something that can begin again."

21

Art rested his bottle on his knee. He took a long look at his friend, then he leaned forward. "Sounds like hope to me."

Brazos Ben let his bottle hover in the air from a lolling hand. "Yeah, I guess you can call it hope. If a man begins again and keeps on beginning again, I guess hope's in there somewhere."

Art remained for a time while they listened to the creatures of the night sing their subtle songs. Then, after downing a paper cup of instant coffee, he departed.

Though the night had worn away, Brazos Ben was not weary. In his restlessness he turned to Johnny Cash, who sang to him from the year 2002, the dying legend giving voice to his melancholy through the lyrics of a younger brooding soul named Trent Reznor, a song called "Hurt." The hermit of the Brazos listened from the cherrywood chair beneath his trophies.

The song awakened a memory. Ben rose and went up to his bedroom. He rummaged through the filing cabinet. At the back of the bottom drawer, he pushed aside a disheveled pile of invoices until he found a shoebox. He put it on the drafting table, donned his reading glasses, and went through the contents.

Toward the bottom of the box, he found a yellowed letter from Raymondville, Texas, to his father, Elijah "Red" Menefee. The envelope bore the postmark February 12, 1946. The letter, from one Dan Loop, began with greetings and news of family. Then a new paragraph began:

"Red, here's the photo for proof your boy was there. It was a big one. Took out my best cow hound before it was over. Tracked it from Olmito all the way up to Old Cavazos. I reckon it's the last one in the Valley, but you never know."

From the envelope, Ben drew out a black-and-white photo. His calloused hands held it as if it were the last lily of summer.

There, surrendered to the slope of the earth in the center of the photo, lay a slain jaguar beneath a Texas wild olive tree. The mouth was open, the eyes blank, the limbs splayed at angles like the branches of the tree from which it had fallen. Men stood nearby with rope, preparing to raise him in display.

Around the body were the faces of Ben's childhood.

There's Tío Rodrigo, wearing the chaps he always wore, the pair studded with conchos. There's his son, Javier, always ready to play. We mixed our English and Spanish until we were speaking "Spanglish!" Ha! And there's Ralph Allen Parker with his spiral-bore shotgun. Even in this black-and-white photo I can see the sunburn on his face. That New Hampshire bride of his never got used to the South Texas sun.

Ben took in the others in the photo as they stood around the jaguar looking at him: people young and old, from north and south of the border, some whose names he remembered, and others, though forgotten by name, who remained known by the memory of their characters and their deeds, which they had impressed like creek beds upon him.

There I am. I'm so short you can barely see me. Looks like Aunt Sal had just given me a haircut. Poor woman, she could never keep me clean for long, I was so rambunctious. 'At least you'll have a clean head, boy!' she'd say. 'If your momma comes down here, I want her to see that at least I tried!' My hair was bright red back then, just like Poppa's. My fiery temperament was just like his too. That's why they called him "Red." But he changed after home fell apart and he sent me to live in the Valley with kinfolk. Yep, he changed. He began again.

Oracle abided in the flying manmachine. Here, as in the barn, he smelled Man, but a new set of smells mingled with it: processed air, coffee, and the ozone of electronics. A Man made his way past the crate toward the cramped quarters of the aft of the plane. His breath smelled of seafood mixed with a lingering cloud of Polo cologne. After the clink of flatware and clunk of cabinets, he passed by again. Oracle heard the chatter of Man through a blast of tones from the plane engines.

"Thanks for the crabcakes, Eddie. What did you put in those?"

"It's called Old Bay seasoning."

"Wow, those were one-bite wonders. We're about to make our descent, so it's just as well that we finished them off along with your deviled eggs. That salmon filling was awesome!"

"Have you made contact with the ground, Tripp?"

"Yeah, Raphael's turned the strip lights off for a test of the homing tech."

"No lights? You mean our landing is also going to be a science experiment?"

"It's one of my new toys, Eddie. You know how I'm always trying out prototypes from my R and D guys. And when we touch down, Raphael will switch the strip lights back on. You'll see 'em right when we land."

"The runway's pretty short, Tripp. It's barely to spec. A night landing with no lights doesn't leave us with much safety margin. What if we don't have enough airstrip?"

"Don't worry, Eddie. Nothing that putting the props into beta range won't take care of. I've got you."

"Have you ever done that before? That 'beta fish' thing?"

"Beta *range*, Eddie. And it's *betta* fish, not *beta* fish. It's not often I get to correct a wordsmith like you. I've landed the plane in beta range a hundred times. Could do it in my sleep."

"Hey, I don't want you sleeping! Let me bring you another energy drink to make sure you're at the peak of your game for this. It's got natural guayusa from the Ecuador rainforest. It's a type of holly sustainably grown by the Kichwa. I hear they drink it to sharpen their dream interpretation skills."

"Interesting. Coulda used that for a dream I had last year… But don't worry about bringing me one now; I'm okay."

"All right then, I'll go back to reading Ovid on my Kindle. It will keep my mind off your—beta range."

"What's an 'Ovid'? Sounds like some kinda virus."

"Now it's my turn to bring you up to speed. Ovid is a *poet*. If you're looking for elegies bathing in love and lament, he's one of the best. He was a Roman who explored many myths and old stories, from creation all the way to Julius Caesar. His magnum opus is called *Metamorphoses*, 'The Transformations.' It's what I'm reading right now."

"Sure, Eddie. Whatever you say. If ancient poetry is your preferred cup of chill, that's fine. As for me, my 'tequila' is technology. The more elegant it is, the better it works on me, kinda like your old Ovid, I guess."

The chatter continued. The engine's droning gradually shifted to a rhythmic throb. There was a gentle shove of gravity forward as the pitch attitude of the plane changed. For a brief moment, Oracle's ears hurt.

Outside, cloud cover pulled back from the moon. She was at the full, the Strawberry Moon of June, and she trimmed the King Air with a galvanized glow just as she had the stakeboard truck that had taken Oracle out of the Valley ten months before.

Inside the cabin, with its lights off, moonlight reached through the windows, gliding over the empty seats where Tripp and Chase had faced one another, discussing the jaguar a summer ago. The moon continued her search as the angle of the plane's descent afforded it. Her beams crossed the floor of the cargo bay, passed through the bars of a crate, and fell upon the eyes of the lord of the Valley. The moon was surprised.

"What are you doing here?"

"The one who wears the Crown of Three Choices has taken me once again, and once again you and I shall see what we shall see."

"How can I serve you this time?"

"Pour out your light just as before, just as you always do in your dance with the sun."

"I will, sire, with joy. Your friends will bathe in the same light I shine on you, just as before."

"That is consolation in my separation from them. Thank you."

And they communed together, enjoying the comfort that comes when affection glows without words or needs in the simple presence of the beloved.

The moon searched for others in the cabin who could also share in the moment, but the one Man present, having laid aside both Kindle and Ovid, was preoccupied with an anxious search of the earth below. The moon kissed his cheek and slipped away.

At 12:50 a.m. on the north side of Eden's Bend, Raphael, the chief ranch hand, stood watchful in deer hunter's camo under an oak. Parked nearby was his ATV and the platform

cart hitched to it. The gravel airstrip shone a pale, glowing gray in the moonlight, cutting a straight path in the branchy darkness that threatened on all sides to cover it again the moment Man stopped taming it. A jackrabbit hopped across.

Raphael heard the King Air. His eyes found the sound, a blinking light descending in the distance. His iPad showed that the homing beacon, anchored on his end of the airstrip, was doing its job, while infrared beams marked the length and width of the strip.

Raphael lifted his walkie-talkie to his mouth. "Looks like she's working down here, gentlemen."

"Roger, we copy," the copilot's voice crackled back. "Signal engaged. Visuals confirmed. Looks like Tripp's gadget works. It's got a great voice, by the way. Sounds like Grace Kelly."

"And how is our special passenger?" Raphael asked.

"Eddie's taking good care of him," answered Tripp. "Haven't heard any complaints from the crate. I bet he's hungry, though. Eddie didn't share our midnight snack with him."

"That's why I'm sticking close to my ATV when you get here…Is the test over? Want me to switch on the lights for the landing strip now?"

"Negative, negative, let's go ahead and try instruments only. I think we're good to land. Switch 'em on when we hit the strip."

"Okay, well copied," Raphael replied. "Hey, I know the app, she's working, but I'm going to turn on my headlights to show you where the gravel ends and trouble begins, just in case. Is that okay? It would make me feel better."

"Sure thing, Raphael. See you in a minute."

The pilots turned their craft southeast for the final approach. In the southern sky, the moon shone on the sleeping forest crowding the landing strip, while to the east, on the Laguna

Madre of the Gulf of Mexico, a cluster of lights clung to the town of Port Mansfield. Beyond the shore, lamplit boats lay anchored in the sea like stars fallen from their constellations.

Inside the cockpit a woman's elegant voice spoke from the console:

"Landing speed green at one hundred knots. Descent rate green at seven hundred feet per minute. Touchpoint in fourteen seconds."

At touchdown, the cushion of air gave way to the jarring of crushed stones. Raphael turned on the strip lights, which ran white then yellow along each side, green at the beginning, and red at the end. Raphael sat at a red corner of the strip in his ATV, its headlights playing their part to illuminate the plane's way.

The Beechcraft's brakes and beta-range props persuaded the plane to halt with plenty of gravel to spare. Beyond it began a forest of mesquite, oak, elm, and ash.

As the King Air wound down, Edwin opened the cargo-bay door. Raphael pulled up the ATV, and together the two moved the aluminum box holding the jaguar. Oracle heard the grunts and hoarse whispers of the Men as they struggled to lower him properly.

"This guy weighs a ton!" whispered Edwin.

"More like two hundred fifty pounds, I'd say." Raphael replied. "That's only an eighth of a ton. But no worries, amigo, just get him to the cart, and the wheels will take care of the rest. I've macheted a path to the release spot."

Raphael and Edwin drove into the forest, the ranch hand at the wheel.

The air of South Texas poured into Oracle's container: the smell of cattle; the sting of engine exhaust; the deep, rugged resins of weather-beaten trees. And there was Man mixed in it all, his scent a vaporous signature of what he had eaten, what he had drunk, and what he desired. Oracle stirred. He stood up in the crate and made a low, steady call until the aluminum vibrated.

"Did you hear that?" Edwin asked. "He sounds famished!"

"Could be hungry to eat or hungry to go free. We will find out which one, won't we?" He playfully slapped Edwin's back. Edwin gave him a sharp look.

"I don't want to find out. I just want to complete this to-do list and delete it as soon as possible. It's so outside of my job description I won't be able to update my LinkedIn profile with it."

Raphael smiled. "Sí, señor, this is what you call a low-profile link to the zoo's lost jaguar."

The Men reached a clearing and halted the vehicle. They unhitched the cart and maneuvered it until an object came into view before Oracle at the window of the crate's door. He saw dressed out venison hanging from a freshly cut branch beside a steel basin of water and a dish of man-made zoo chow. On a tripod beside these, a small box with a dark glass eye watched him. He heard the electronic whine of the manmachine engines as they came to life again back at the airstrip. The Man in camo tied a cord to a ring just above the door of the crate.

"Come on, Raphael! Let's go!" Edwin urged as he assumed the driver's seat. The plane engines throbbed. Raphael walked backward a few steps, unraveling a spool of the cord until he climbed into the ATV and pulled the cord taut.

Before Oracle, the door complained with a clarion wail as it opened. The shadow-bands of the barred window pulled away from his face, giving him a clear view of the food and water waiting for him before the glass eye. The jaguar dropped his forepaws onto a carpet of Indiangrass. The black tip of his tail brushed the crate behind him farewell.

Raphael tossed the spool to the ground. "¡Vamanos!"

Edwin wheeled the ATV around and sped to the plane. Once there, he hopped out, and Raphael returned to the driver's seat.

"¡Adios, señor!" He shook Edwin's hand with haste. "I'll go now. Don't want to be hanging around when the jaguar goes hunting!"

Edwin returned to the King Air, springing up the stepladder as if it was hot iron, hoisting his body into a standing position within the cargo bay. The plane lurched under the force of the brakes holding it back as the pilots throttled up. Edwin pulled in the stepladder and thrust it into its socket in the cargo-bay door above. He grasped the handle, the muscles in his wiry arm straining to close it as quickly as possible. The wheels rolled in sudden relief from the brakes, and Edwin was still strapping himself into a seat when the plane lifted. The King Air soared above the waters of the Laguna Madre.

As the plane climbed, Edwin was misty-eyed, although he could not have explained to you exactly why if you had asked.

It's fear, but I'm not afraid. It's a restless conscience, but not a guilty one. I'm not remorseful but glad to play a part in this collusion. Maybe it's... 'joy'?

"Farewell, cat," he whispered as he looked out the window. "I'm glad you're free. And your rosette spots...I think they were just beginning to tell me something. They were each like a dollop on a painter's palette. Colors for blank canvas! I shall miss them!"

And for the rest of the night Edwin considered how a single spot of creation, as simple as a snowflake or lily pad or dry desert bush, could transform into the first chapter of a story that might take a whole lifetime to read.

—ᴟ—

The sound of the flying manmachine receded until the night sky was still. At the zenith, the stars Vega, Altair, and Deneb, guardians of the Summer Triangle, watched while the constellations of the eagle and the swan circled them. In the southeast, Mars honored what he beheld below, and likewise Jupiter in the southwest, while almost due south Saturn did the same alongside the ripe Strawberry Moon.

The points of the Triangle above paralleled the points of the tripod below, where its legs supported the camera eye of Man. Oracle stood before the tripod. He drank from the basin. And as he did, the heavens gathered round him there—swan, stars, eagle, planets, and the argent disc of the moon. All of them met him with their reflections, surrounding him on the surface of the water, dancing with the ripples his whiskers made on the liquid mirror.

Oracle saw that the moon was smiling. He looked up at her. She glowed brightly as she spoke.

"Welcome back, Lord of the Valley. Welcome to the land where the Lonely Tree has become the Lovely Tree by your breath bathed in my light. Welcome to the realm of forgotten names where Kahoo's prayer still whispers in the wind, calling upon me and the stars to watch and wait with open eyes. And behold, we have!

Until another comes to lead the kingdom
From the north and from the sky
From here to river's end!

Yes, from the north *and from the* sky
From here to river's end!

31

4

GREETING THE FORGETFUL

Oracle drank the water to its last drop, dry as his mouth had become in the crate of the King Air. He ate the venison, and his tongue bathed in essences of wild rye and bluestem grass, of sun-drenched berries and hidden creeks. He smelled the zoo chow, a pile of identical shapes in a plastic dish, shapes whose propylene glycol preservative was a petrochemical relative of the polymers in the dish itself. Nonetheless, there was some good in the zoo chow. So, Oracle ate it after a long, pondering inspection.

The lord of the Valley stretched his forelimbs while his haunches pressed the earth. He arched his back high, all paws claw-anchored, body rising like a wind-filled sail on stiff lines. Every sinew in his body thanked him as he took in a deep breath.

One chapter of life is complete and another has begun. The days of drowsy sameness and safety have passed. The days of possibilities and peril have come. I cannot have the one without the other.

He journeyed into the forest. Oak, elm, and Rio Grande ash welcomed him, as did the ubiquitous mesquite. The essential oils of the trees effused the air with aromas made precious by the slow, silent labor required to produce them in the current trial of drought. The trees awakened Oracle's senses: sight, smell, sound, touch, taste, and that unnamed sense that blends them together. Buffalo grass kissed his paws in a way the smooth surface of the aluminum crate could never have done.

The kiss reminds me of the grasses of Sian Ka'an. But I perceive the drought in their blades.

Dawn came as a lavender sea. A battleship of a cloud anchored in the east, and light burned from its crenulated edges. The moon, glowing on the southwest horizon, bade her friend farewell.

On the ground between the grasses, Oracle saw the tracks of grazing animals.

They are clearly relatives of those I know in the Yucatán, yet they are not the same. They are oddly sized and curve in a way I have not seen before. They call upon what I know, but they signal something not yet known.

Oracle gave the call of territory, a series of short, cough-like roars. The jaguar, hearing no call in reply and finding no tracks, scratches, or scat among the trees to serve notice that he was in another big cat's territory, continued deeper into the unknown realm. The sun's first beam, skipping across the sea, alighted upon the tree leaves around him and turned them from gray to green.

I shall find water, for there, I shall also find those who live here and can tell me of this place. It is the manrealm of South Texas, to be sure, but I do not know the story of this portion of it. Wait…the scent of those who chew the cud reaches me.

The cat of Sian Ka'an followed the scent, cleared a stand of cedar elms, and found himself on the edge of a meadow. On the other side were antlered animals nibbling on mesquite leaves.

Perhaps these are the ones who made the strange tracks I saw.

Oracle considered the most prominent one, whose stern head stood upon a neck both sturdier and longer than that of the nimble deer of Sian Ka'an. The broad chest bore a bristling coat of arms, hairs as stiff as brushes ascending alongside pale marks. Upon his head was a crown Oracle had never seen before: dark antlers spiraling gracefully upward in curve after curve as if in slow dance with the wind.

The South African kudu turned toward Oracle, for his ears and nose had told him of the cat's arrival. He grunted in displeasure. At the sound, all turned. A half-dozen impala stood stock still, their ribbed antlers branching out like great goal posts, their eyes white with fear, pairing with the white that trimmed their heads. Thomson's gazelles, with their spike-like horns and signature black stripe along their bodies, pressed themselves into a tight group in defensive stance.

With a stomp the kudu turned and fled. The impala scattered like arrows shot from six bows, and the gazelles disappeared into the brush with a single spring of their nimble legs.

A lone oryx, horns long and straight like javelins, remained. With face fixed on Oracle, he backed up for every step the jaguar moved forward until his hindquarters touched the leaves of a thicket. With a sudden, clumsy turn made more unwieldy by the horns, the oryx fled, crashing through a barrier of dry and brittle branches.

Oracle crossed the meadow and entered a grove of mesquite and live oak. The bramble beneath them was thick, but he found a way through, as all cats do, as green growth and drought struck stems worked with his rosette spots to cloak him from sight.

What is that strange scent I perceive: A horse? A donkey? It is like them, but it is neither.

Peering ahead through the tangled mass of undergrowth, Oracle spied a coat pattern of animals he had never seen.

Their stripes confound my eyes. They shift with the shapes in the thicket before me. Branch, blade, and stripe all mingle. It is hard to tell which is which.

One of the beasts raised his voice in the direction of the bramble. "Who's there? Your odor has betrayed your stealth. Are you one of *us* or one of *them*?"

"Who are 'us' and who are 'them'?" Oracle replied from his hidden place. "Do you mean your fleet-footed friends with the solemn horns? Do you mean Man? Tell me the story that made such a divided state in your dry and thick-wooded realm that all must be 'us' or 'them.'"

"You act ignorant on purpose to fool us!" the second one accused. "Did you not get here like we did? Did you not suffer the bars and boats of Men? The gates by water and by land?"

"My gate was from the air. I came here from the south until Man pierced me with sleep and took me to the north. I escaped only to be brought low under the paw of a ghost cat. Man brought me back from Death's door and carried me in his machine of unbroken wings through the air. Then he brought his machine down to noisy stones and set me free here."

The first one snorted. "You feign a ruse while your pack surrounds us! Of course there's only one way in here. Why do you lie and make it sound as if you know nothing? We will be nobody's fool. No one can come in but by the way *we* came in. Your question shows your deception toward us."

The cat of the Yucatán reclined inside the hedge, as yet unseen to his interrogators, considering the optical illusion of the stripes. "If you choose to think my question a deception, then no number of words will clear the brush between us. Were I to say I am from 'them,' I would not know if I were telling the truth, for I do not know who 'they' are. And were I to say I am one of 'you,' whoever you are, you would not believe me either. I would not even believe myself, for I do not know who you are.

I am from above
That is what is true
Tell me what you know
I will then tell you

The second one brayed. "A fool we are to share anything with you, marsh-scented stranger! We were here before you, and we have a right to require an answer: Who *are* you? Answer quickly. Are you one of *us* or one of *them*?"

Oracle considered the question. "I am neither. I am a visitor to your land. I come from above."

The first one neighed in laughter. "From above! Do you take us for wobbly legged colts who believe everything they hear? We know fur when we smell it. There's not a single feather on your body. We can tell from here! You are all water and root and fish in your scent. Venison too! Get lost, we command! Get lost!"

Twigs snapped and leaves crunched as the bellowing striped sentries backed into the brush behind them.

"I cannot get there," Oracle said.

"Get where?" asked the second one. "What do you mean you cannot 'get there'?"

"I cannot find the way to Lost, for I have not forgotten my name."

The first one snorted. "Strange answers you give, as strange as your smell. Give us then your name."

"I am the jaguar Oracle of Sian Ka'an in the manrealm called the Yucatán. I will come out from the thicket and show you."

"We don't care to see you!" the second one shouted, and more undergrowth protested under a scurry of retreating hooves. "We don't give the fuzz of a wild peach to know *anything* about you if you are not one of us. For if you are not one of us, who knows what you will do to us, and who knows who you really are? A lion? A cheetah? Such is your smell but soaked in sweat and the swamp water of an alien realm! We care nothing for them, and we care nothing for you, too, if you belong to them. We care for nothing except that you leave us to ourselves."

Oracle silently approached the edge of the bushes. There they were: heads donkey-like in shape, manes stiff as scouring brushes, round barrel bodies on stocky legs, striped head to toe: two zebras from Tanzania. Oracle left the leaves behind and appeared to them.

The zebras' eyes widened with fear and their long ears flattened back in dismay. The one on the right swung left, while the one on the left swung right, and both zebras struck one another with a thud of such force they fell back in opposite directions, rolling on the ground. They scrambled to their feet and galloped away, one east and one west, in long curves leading back to one another far behind the scrub. Nothing remained before Oracle but an unhurried cloud of dust.

—⟡—

The rhinoceros heard the jaguar was coming, for the zebras, wild with terror, had fled to the shallow middle of a drought-weary pond where the rhinoceros was drinking amid a cloud of flies.

"A mighty cat! Oh, a mighty cat!" the first zebra cried out. "Did you see his fangs?"

"I saw nothing but his face lit with the morning sun," said the second one. "Its brightness was like fire and forced me to run!"

"Certainly there are fangs behind that great mouth of his."

"Oh yes, certainly! A great mouth hides great fangs, no doubt! It's good we ran, and it's good we keep running!"

"Yes, let's gallop to the feeding trough! It's close to the manplace. Man will protect us there. Yes, he will!"

The rhinoceros swung his great head around, and with it the great curved horn and the lesser spike behind it. He grunted in annoyance at the panicking beasts. "So 'zebra' of you to go on at the mouth! Why the commotion? Scared of the half-starved kittens native to here? You're disgusting in your quaking striped hide: a skin that's thin, not thick like mine. If your dreaded 'mighty cat' comes, I will run right at him, for that is my name: Charge. I fear no one, for no one can get through to me. No one overcomes my horns."

"To each his own!" the first zebra called out. "As for us, our place is by the trough! Well-fed means fuel for courage, as we say. Best of luck to you! Farewell!"

The zebras splashed their way to shore and made a fading wet path to a feeding station where Man kept watch in air-conditioned comfort.

The rhinoceros reflected on what he had heard, as still as a statue except for his ears, which flicked away flies. The flies had heard every word too, but they were unintimidated by the news of fear.

"Ha!" Charge said. "If anything, the news doubles their numbers. Fear holds the promise of fresh flesh to feast on. Hmm, and speaking of feast, I'm a little hungry. Until that feline thing gets here, let me try some of those pink flowers. The white-tailed deer call them 'rockrose.' They sure are sweet. Like the brandybush where I'm from."

Charge enjoyed the rockrose bush, which flourished in the sun just beyond the shade of live oak and Texas mountain laurel trees. His dexterous upper lip probed like a searching finger for the tenderest leaves. He foraged. He flicked flies.

"Let's see what kind of sport this cat might make," he whispered to the bush.

Oracle drew near the pond. Seeing the variety of animal tracks in the mud around the water, he made a careful survey of them. Twice he circled the pond. Then he also found a bed of rockrose to sit among. He cleaned his paws of the ungrateful mud that had gathered there, stretching out the toes of each foot until the skin between them, clothed in downy fur, stretched to the full. He licked each toe with a tender tongue.

The rhino saw and took several steps, dropping each foot with a threatening thud. Oracle continued to placidly clean his paws, tranquilly allowing the ground's vibrations to pass through him as Charge approached. The rhinoceros stood pointing his horn toward the unwelcome guest.

"Who are you?" he said in a tone as flat as the bottom of his feet, each of which supported the beast through a thick pad beneath three great toes. And yet, relative to his massive girth, each leg was somewhat small, like a sapling supporting too many branches. Nevertheless, Charge stood as solidly as if he had never moved from that one spot of lonely earth. The cat spoke to the exiled king.

"I am the jaguar Oracle of Sian Ka'an."

The rhino scraped the ground and snapped his tail. "Why are you here?"

"Man set me free. I explore this unknown realm that I have been given."

"It is unknown to me too, for I am not from this realm either. Man surrounded me and lifted me out of my home to be here. I spent a moon on a vast realm of water called The Sea to reach this place. I was barred into a box like the beasts of Man that serve him. Then he brought me here, where I roam at will, alone but free."

Oracle rose, his tail brushing the bushes. "I follow the trail left for me in the prayer of my ancestor Kahoo the Grave, who perished seventy springs ago. He was the last lord of the Valley. I have come to pick up the trail from the place he left off and follow it to river's end."

The rhino lifted his head, looking down at him through small but imperious eyes.

"So you say, but I have a question for you. If I say *I* am the lord of the Valley now, how would you answer that? For no other living thing on four feet is as strong as I am here, and strength has the final say about who is lord of whom on this earth."

The cat of rosette spots noticed a stray piece of mud and licked it off. "Strength has a voice indeed on this earth, but does it truly have the final say? The first story does not speak it so. The first story speaks a different tale. It says that the story itself—that first story—is itself the final say. The first and the last."

The rhino squared his shoulders in the face of the cat of the Southern Jungle. "You speak a foreign language to me. I am suspicious. What could be more final than *strength*? What could be stronger than the *will* to use it unafraid? My name is Charge, and I shall show you, yea, I shall prove it to you. I shall block your way and show you that the story you claim as 'first' is second to strength. Strength can trample the story and forge a new path."

The cat of the Ones Who Remember reclined, head on a limb—though his claws were out. "But if the first story formed the earth you stand on, then will not the path your horn forges bring you back to it in the end? For the story is not a tale only. It is the whole realm in which we live. You cannot go outside of it. For not even the Maker himself lives outside of it. He himself, who spoke the story and made Man the Namer, lives in the story. There is no other path to find."

The rhino grunted, throwing his head at a rockrose bush, which he caught in the crook between his great horn and the smaller one behind it. He tore out the rockrose and tossed it away. "Your words are a tangle of vines for my feet. Come here, and I will show you what has the final word: your story or my strength. I will show you the weakness of your words."

Charge threw up his tail straight into the air. He withdrew until he was a stone's throw away, turned, and snorted, sending dust up from the ground like a puff of smoke. He marked the earth with his foot. Then he charged, lowering his double-horned gouger on a collision course with the cat of the House of Panthera Onca.

Oracle hopped to a mountain laurel branch, and Charge brandished his horn below. The jaguar looked upon him, seeing the rhino's head within paw's reach as he had the bull of Bear Claw Ranch.

"It is not a time to strike, but to breathe," said the lord of the Valley.

And so he did, long and steady and unhurried, as unhurried as a seed of the baobab tree, which, though for a season appears to sleep the sleep of death, has been living and growing all along within the still and silent shell cradling the tender plant. His breath descended as if it were an unseen dew, an early morning mist in the bright midday.

The rhino felt a strange new air about him like the cool breeze preceding rare rains in the rugged savannah that had been his home on the edge of the Kalahari. His anger cooled too, yet the fear of the cat's fangs lingered, a fear whispering "What if I am wounded? What if I am undone? What if I am led astray?" But the fears, though real, did not have the final say.

"Look at that!" Charge said. "The branch you sit on—the whole tree—it's blooming! The smell of the blossoms makes the air smell thick with something sweeter than grapes!"

"Yes, and more than just the fruit of the day," Oracle replied. "This is the air of a different vintage. An older bloom. The first one."

Charge ceased speaking, for the aroma arrested him, making the protests on his tongue—a tongue which had bullied far more foes than his horn—seem oddly immature.

It seems to me now that to bully this cat with my horn and my tongue would be the kind of thing only a young punk would do. Why would I go back to that? The mature thing is to be still, for I am no longer the center. If I'm really brave like I boast, I will be still. I choose courage.

The breath lingered over Charge, settled, and sank through his calloused hide until it reached his heart. He relaxed his shoulders, and as he did, he returned his horn to rest, placed his great hulk of a body on the ground, and reclined among the rockrose. Oracle dropped to the ground.

Charge looked at the cat. The shining rays of the morning gilded his red-gold spotted coat and illuminated the white trim of his body and mouth.

This is a calm I did not see in the cats of the Kalahari, nor in the felines native to this South Texas realm.

And as he looked, a memory came to him, filling him like the rising water within the pierced compartments of a proud ironclad.

—⚜—

Adam was returning from the mangrove orchard, where the trees grew in water up to his knees. Their roots sang as they sank into the fresh earth; their branches lifted up their arms in adoration of the Maker. Adam journeyed the whole day through his garden estate, ascending forests of fruit trees on steep hills until he came out on a wide plain of low bushes and flowers.

Adam stood amazed. "The air of this field is thick with promises, invisible but for the way the green blades of grass bow and whisper a throng of songs to my Father, who planted them."

In the golden orb of the setting sun, Adam's keen and unblemished eye saw on the horizon's edge yet another new creature. It was grazing. Adam walked toward the animal and reached it after the sun had sunk and the first stars were appearing.

Hearing his approach, the great animal lifted its head to reveal a horn like that of a mountain peak. He turned and approached the Namer, for the Maker had told him that today was the day he would receive his name.

Adam smiled. He placed his right hand upon the horn.

Protector you are
Here under the stars
Defender you are
Yet gentler than Mars

Pathfinder you are
A way to the sun
Split open the fire
And give life a run

—⚬—

"I remember," the rhinoceros whispered. "I remember what he said. What Adam said to the first of my kind."

"You remember," said the lord of the Valley.

"Yes, I do. Thank you."

Oracle walked to the uprooted rockrose, retrieved it with a gentle mouth, and placed it before the rhinoceros.

"You would do well to replant her," said Oracle, "for her root still lives, and therefore her story."

The rhinoceros bowed. "With the help of the tunnel folk, I will, sire."

His strength now armored with the great calm of the first story, Paladin the rhinoceros watched Oracle depart through the leafy veil of oak and laurel, a place where their boughs and branches mingled. After he had gone, Paladin moved to that place.

"I will rest here, for I have work to do. Work inside my hide."

And there Paladin rewrote the tale he had told himself during a life of survival far from the breath of Eden.

"That story is over. A new one has begun."

And as he finished, the tunnel folk appeared, members of the House of Geomys whom Man calls the Texas pocket gopher.

"Hail to you, Keeper of the Great Horn," a gopher said. "The lord of the Valley sent us. He breathed on us, and we are no longer afraid. You are not a stranger. You are our neighbor. How can we help you?"

With the help of the tunnel folk, Paladin replanted the rockrose. And she took root and began again.

5

At the Launch Pad

On Oracle's first morning back at Eden's Bend, Chase watched the dawn reflect off the reservoir for the launchpad while she sat in the seat of her rolling walker. Her jeep was a stone's throw behind her, and from it were the tracks of shuffling feet between wheels leading up to where she was. The jaguar was far to the north in the four-hundred-square-mile realm, while she was at its southern end, where the soft gold of the early morning sky colored the man-made pool. Beneath her feet bluestem grass flourished from the seepage of the reservoir through seams in the cement to the soil around it. Nearby slept the rocket thrusters, suspended cauldrons awaiting their combustible brew. The blast pit dropped beneath the thrusters, silent but bearing the scorching memory of the recent engine test.

Chase sank back in the walker seat. She considered the reservoir.

"So little water to go around," she whispered, "while this place drinks it all."

Her eyes caught sight of two Harris hawks rising from dying oaks. She followed them as they worked together, circling the rocket then banking away in search of prey. As they returned to the oaks, the sound of a walking horse reached her, then a voice. "Happy Friday!" She swiveled the walker.

Tripp swaggered in the saddle under a cowboy hat. "So, getting a little contemplation time in before our conversation, I see."

Chase flushed in frustration but held her tongue. Tripp clicked a guiding command to his horse.

"You always were the reflective type before Lovers' Leap, but the miracle of surviving that crazy plunge of yours seems to have hard-wired it into you all the more!"

"I'm thankful to be alive," she said dryly. "In light of a lifetime, six months of recovery is a small thing. I'm just grateful I have breath to begin with."

Tripp tapped the walker with his riding crop. "I'll say! I still can't believe how lucky you were to survive a topple like that! Limestone doesn't normally break anyone's fall; it breaks *them*. You couldn't have targeted a better cushion of brush at the bottom than the one you found when you fell face up. Now here you are in one piece with the help of wheels until you walk again."

He smiled. She turned away, scanning the dry creek bed beyond the launchpad.

Tripp dismounted. "I'll let my ride enjoy the same grassy oasis my old horse was grazing when I found him here." And he tied the animal's lead on a corkscrew stake he twisted into the ground.

Chase, eyes on the empty creek, paid no attention to him when he returned. He tapped her shoulder with two fingers and offered a warm handshake, but there was no warm return. Her eyes stared into his like torches cornering a fugitive in a cave. Tripp raised his eyebrows, withdrew his hand, and took off his hat as he let out a sigh of disappointment.

"I can see you're not happy, and I don't blame you." He nodded his head toward the launchpad sound buffer system, which pumped hundreds of thousands of gallons of water into the blast zone to dampen the engines' deafening roar. "Those runoff pipes ruined the creek, and even those Harris hawks are frustrated since mice can't reach the reservoir like they did the riverbed. Yeah, I made a mess, I admit it. I put the restoration of the creek on the task list the same week we talked about it on the plane back in August. I didn't forget. But, as you can see, we haven't made much progress."

Chase fumed. "You haven't made *any* progress. Practically speaking, you have forgotten. The hawks and the horses have done more to restore this place than you have!"

Tripp put a fist on his hip. "Chase, I hear ya, we've got a job to do that will land us such a boon of funding that there will be more than enough to reconstruct the creek. I promise we'll make it a little paradise for field mice and Harris hawks alike. Critters from all over South Texas will gather to drink the water and enjoy their breakfast. And what we do to restore this creek will be a model for what we can for every other creek on Eden's Bend. It just takes money, Chase. Be patient."

Chase squinted her eyes at him and pursed her lips. "I know your tagline to make up for this grief. 'Money can go a long way in getting us back to Eden.' You don't have to remind me."

Tripp gave an audible exhale. "Well, if you don't need me to remind you, then why did you call me out here first thing in the morning? My team already sent you a report of their inspection. It will take a *six-digit figure* to course-correct the creek before next month's test launch."

"We're in trouble, Tripp."

"I *know* we're in trouble, Chase, and I know our troubles will double if someone outside the project learns about it before we fix it, whether that's the government or go-green activists. Shoot, I've already heard about a group of zealous college kids planning to visit us and 'inspect' our ostrich farm."

"No, Tripp, you're not listening. You don't get who I mean when I say 'we.' I'm not talking about IT Menefee Incorporated and its image management campaign. I'm talking about those Harris hawks and all the wild animals they represent. I'm talking about those oaks close to death and all the green things they groan for. Tripp, pull back on your projects for *their* sake. Halt them until this drought stops or your beloved R & D guys can solve the problem of how this place is going to find water while you pour what precious little of it there is into high-tech visions!"

Tripp squatted beside the walker, bumping it with his knee on his way down.

"Sorry." He picked a blade of grass and paused, watching the Harris hawks preening side by side on the dying oak. Then they lifted their wings and flew away together.

"Pull back on my projects, huh? That's a tall order."

Chase reached from her seat—the pain of the move slowing her—and plucked the grass from him. "You're no stranger to tall orders, Mr. Menefee. You smuggled my lost jaguar down here last night, didn't you?"

Tripp chuckled. "'*My* lost jaguar?'"

Chase clicked her tongue sharply and rolled her eyes. "*Our* lost jaguar, okay? Sorry!"

"*Ours* for sure," he said as he grinned. "I haven't slept since I flew him down here. I puddle-jumped the King Air over to Harlingen and came right back for our sunrise consultation—Hey, you gotta watch the video Raphael just sent me from the jaguar's release site—But what's your point? Wasn't it the plan all along to set him free here one day? Your zoo was just the holding pen. Sure, the cottonwood broke him out of jail and my dad bailed him out of trouble, but those two just sped things up; it was still the plan."

"That's true, but, Tripp, you have major industries and exotic animals affecting the native environment in an unprecedented way. There's so much going on that we don't know how introducing an apex predator into the mix is going to affect the balance of everything—especially in this severe drought. It's the same as flying your King Air on empty to see how far it can go on fumes!"

Tripp scrunched his mouth. He lowered his voice but raised its intensity, putting a hand on an arm of the rolling walker to stabilize his squat.

"I distinctly remember you using that figure of speech before. 'We're running on empty' while I build the airplane in the air."

"That's right." She nodded matter-of-factly.

Tripp leaned closer to Chase and lowered his voice to a whispered growl. "But I also distinctly remember telling you I brought you on this project to be my copilot, not my air traffic control!"

"And I told you I *am* being your copilot. If you want to fly solo, just hand me the parachute. But if you really want my input, here it is again for the thousandth time: Data, Tripp, data! You're flying by the seat of your pants. Do you know where that saying comes from?"

"What, 'seat of your pants?' It means 'go with your gut,' right?"

"More your butt than your gut. In the pioneer days of aviation, before there were reliable instruments, pilots would feel where the pressure was on their bottoms with the seat to figure out their angle in the air. 'Pitch' and 'roll' is what they were feeling, like the bubbles in a carpenter's level. How would you like to learn that you're nose diving because you can't feel the seat anymore? That's exactly what you're doing! Tripp, look, there's just not enough water and not enough research. Without both, your six simultaneous 'special initiatives' are going to wreak havoc on what you've already got, animals included."

Tripp scoffed, stood, and kicked a stray creek stone as he looked down, but Chase placed a firm hand on his elbow to turn him toward her.

"We're on the same team, Tripp, but I feel like you hide behind the big talk of 'vision' because it's easier than facing the real needs of today. Real things to nurture. Real things within reach. Are you brave enough to care for what you already touch?"

Chase caught her breath, and Tripp found she had a surprised look on her face. She yanked her hand away from his arm.

Tripp cocked his head. "Um, are we still talking about the same thing, or did you just change the subject?"

Chase paused for a moment, shook off the look of surprise, and regained composure. Gently, and with a look of resolute focus, she returned her hand to his arm.

"I'm helping you, Tripp. Consider the benefits of slowing down. I'm not advising you to abandon your developments, I'm advising you to *respect* them. Halt what you can, slow down the rest, and wait for rain. That's all."

Tripp studied her face. Though she blinked as if shooing away a distracting thought, she remained poised in elegant resolve.

Tripp's shoulders relaxed as he let out a sigh. "Your way is like that rain you're talking about. Both have a calming effect on me—though there's a hint of thunder in your voice too!"

He smiled. She returned it.

Tripp looked toward the oaks. In the place where the Harris hawks had been, a neotropic cormorant was now keeping watch.

Tripp frowned inquisitively. "That cormorant seems to be on to our talk. I suppose it's in his interest to restore this creek too. No minnows in the launchpad reservoir."

The prince of Eden's Bend looked the rocket up and down. "She's an expensive dream…and a compelling one, but… yes, Chase, you're right. It's like one of my old roommates at UT used to say after joining the Special Forces, 'Slow is smooth and smooth is fast.' It's the best way to move forward. Thanks for taking my blinders off. I'll give my senior leads a heads-up today. They're already tapping the brakes anyway because tomorrow's Friday, and a lot of folks are leveraging their PTO to make a long holiday out of next week's Fourth of July. Falls on Wednesday this year. Come to think of it, that works for good too with the timing of slowing things down, since they'll already be coasting from the holiday. You sure are sharp with your timing in taking me on!"

Chase grinned. "Yes, I had thought about the timing of our talk."

Tripp gave her a fist bump. "Give me two weeks to park each project in a good place and pay people what I owe them."

"Thank you, Tripp."

Chase rose with difficulty. Tripp steadied her as she moved and placed her hands on the handles of the rolling walker. Together they slowly returned to her jeep, where he helped her into the driver's seat. As he did, the locket on her necklace swung out, catching Tripp's attention. He leaned with a hand on the jeep's door, which was still open.

"Tell me about that locket, Chase. You always wear it. Family heirloom? I can tell from the patterns on the silver that it's got a story."

Chase gently touched the locket, feeling the lapis lazuli stone in its center and the contours encircling it. "Yes, this locket has a story. My story."

51

Tripp watched the eyes of the Cheyenne chief's daughter behold something only she could see. He spoke softly. "Tell me your story."

"My parents named me Chasing Eagle because of the good omen on the day that preceded my birth: An eagle chased away an owl from a tree in our front yard."

"But aren't owls a good sign, too?"

"It depends on the owl and it depends on where you are in the world. To us Northern Cheyenne, the owl is a messenger of death."

"Oh. My mom used to collect little owl statues and fridge magnets. She said they reminded her of wisdom and the like."

"That's true for her tribe, I suppose, but not for mine."

"I see. Then it was a good omen the eagle chased the owl away."

"Yes, eagles are a sign of courage from heaven."

"So, courage from heaven…chasing away death, right?"

"Yes. Or…with how things turned out…working together for good the death that came."

"Hmm. So, something bad happened."

"Mom died."

"What? Oh, man, I'm so sorry. Right away? Like, when you were a baby?"

"No, on my tenth birthday. Mom and Dad and I had a beautiful life up until then. I'm thankful for those ten years. It's ten times more than we would have had if we hadn't ever been."

"That's deep, Chase. I never would have thought of it that way. You put a silver lining in your sadness."

"Well, for Dad and me, it's not just a positive thought. It's true."

"You mean, like a fact."

"Of course. Do you think I would make it through life if I based it on what I feel?"

"Good point. That wisdom applies to almost everything. You put your feelings inside the fact that you, your mom, and your dad enjoyed ten good years. It's like putting furniture in a home. There's real comfort in the home that way."

Chase nodded. "And speaking of home, on the morning my parents brought me to it, the mountain bluebirds sang in that same tree where the eagle chased the owl away. Springtime and summer for ten years, the bluebirds gathered there each sunrise and sang."

Tripp cupped his chin in a thoughtful pose. "That's beautiful."

Chase rested her hands in her lap. "It was. The eagle and the bluebirds were a sign from *Ma'hēō'o*."

"Who?"

"The Creator."

"I see. That's a pretty high-level sign. Did your parents think about naming you 'Sign from the Creator' or 'God Song,' something like that?"

"No, the name of the Creator is too sacred to be placed in a person's name in our tribe. But the sign was the gift he gave, so they named me after the gift: Chasing Eagle. It was my cousins who nicknamed me Chase."

"Hey, there's a point we have in common. My cousins named me Tripp. My full name is a mouthful: Travis McPherson Menefee III. My folks freighted as much family history as they could into my name. I'm a seventh-generation Texan—or, 'Texian,' I guess could say. That's what we called ourselves during the Texas Revolution and the time of the Republic. I think the Mexican dictator Santa Ana just called us 'rebels,' along with a few colorful words to spice it up."

Chase pulled the seatbelt across and buckled it. "My tribe has a name others called us, too."

"What's that?"

"Cheyenne."

"But that's your *name*. You are the Cheyenne."

"That's the name outsiders gave us. French traders, to be exact, when they heard the Sioux tribe speak of us."

"Well then, what do you call yourselves?"

"We call ourselves Tsitsistas: 'the people.'" Chase closed the jeep door and rolled down the window as she started that car.

Tripp gave a puzzled look. "Hmm, tsee... tsee... stahs? You might need to give me a few pronunciation lessons to get that down."

"Not bad for the first try. But 'Cheyenne' is fine. When we say it, we know we are speaking of 'our people.'"

"Right." Tripp stepped back, hands on his hips. "Hey, thanks again for the wake-up call. Not many go toe-to-toe with me. I have a reputation for winning every argument."

"I know." Chase looked at him with a victorious grin as she raised the window to just below her eyes.

The conquered Texian chuckled. "I've got some real whiz kids in my R & D department. I'll shoulder tap the best of them to focus on one project only: a sustainable water supply for Eden's Bend. I'll give them a blank slate to work with: atmospheric water rigs, desalinization, aquifer sounding, whatever it takes. No Eden is complete without a river. One way or another, we'll make one."

He tipped his hat, and the woman nodded farewell.

6

Patch's First Poem

While Chase and the prince of Eden's Bend explored possibilities on the first morning of the jaguar's return, Paco enjoyed his friends at the corral. The next day, he led them to his home, the turquoise trailer. At a point early on in the ten months of this custom, Tío José had ceased to tether the horse, for he freely remained nearby without it. The animals always calmly abided in the vicinity of the trailer with the boy. Sometimes he played in the shade of the canopy, where the folding chairs and fan faithfully served their family. Sometimes he played in the shade of the sunflowers bordering Tío's pumpkin patch, a plot of well-tended earth catty-corner behind Tío and Tía's chairs. Today, Paco played near his foster parents as they sat in the breeze of the rattling fan.

Patch knelt beside the boy the birds named Miracle, watching the manchild's game of marbles with complete attention.

Bog rested in a basin of shallow water beneath the truck bumper, thankful for the personal pool Tía Lourdes had given him, but wary of the immense tires and the foreboding underside of the manmachine, which hung over him like the roof of the mouth of a sleeping dragon.

"This was the last thing many a noble ancestor saw in this life," Bog muttered. And he sang odes to his ancestors in the heat of the late June day.

Paco poured the contents of cold water bottles sloppily into his uplifted mouth, for in so doing not a little splashed over face, head, and hair.

This is good water. It washes away the salty waves where I could not say goodbye, and it washes away the dust from the days beneath the trees.

The child carefully aimed his finger at a marble. He flicked it, and the marbles danced. Again and again he played, but he did not grow weary of the hot weather or the game, nor did the marbles. The boy looked up at Tío and Tía, who smiled as they sipped Mexican limonada, where limes and a dash of salt took the sugar and lemons to the next level. Paco returned the smile.

"Tío! Tía! Look! I poured water on the thirsty ground. It said '¡Gracias!' and drank it all, every last drop. Now the ground is even and smooth. The marbles love it! See how they find each other and make a new dance every time, just like when I played with them at Papá Eli's house, where the fish of many colors swam in bright blue water, and just like when I played with them in Mérida while Mamá made dinner. The marbles have found a new home!"

Tía Lourdes sipped her limonada. "That's a good word, 'home.' Better than 'house.' Houses are many; *homes* are few. You have made our house a home, mijo."

Paco laughed. "I *found* a home, I didn't *make* one! You were already here!"

Tío José smiled. "Sí, but maybe both are true. We *are* a home, but you made it a home indeed. You fulfilled a longing your tía and I have had for years but thought was lost. You have sweetened our lives like the mesquite honey she mixes in the bread she bakes. You have strengthened us too. I almost feel young again." He took his wife's hand.

The horse scratched an itch with the truck's rearview mirror, exhaling noisily.

Paco laughed at the sight. "Thank you for letting my friends stay with me while I play. They like their new house, the barn, but they want to be here instead. It is, as you say, a home not a house. My friends are at home here."

Tío José opened a hand toward the boy. "They are at home here because they are at home with *you*. It is a mystery I do not understand, but I know peace when I see it, and there is peace here. There is *la paz*. I should not trouble that."

"Sí," said Tía Lourdes, "Let *la paz* remain as a welcome guest! We will make a place in our home for you and your friends even if it is something we do not have words for. Whatever adds to the peace of our home is welcome, and *who*ever too. Your friends are welcome here as much as you are."

Paco gathered his marbles for a new game. "We go together, my friends, the marbles, and me."

"Yes, you do," said Tío José. "Somehow the togetherness is itself the peace…But come now, enough talk at the edge of what we have words for, be it English or Spanish. Let's eat! Today is a special day at the chow house, a Friday feast: oak-smoked meats from the ranch's own herd and the ranch's own barbecue pit! And better yet, it's real beef today! Real cattle! No brisket from the ostrich or the emu, bless them." He shook his head as he patted his wife's hand.

She chuckled and shook her own head too. "I know we normally eat fish on Fridays, but this is a heaven-sent exception, I'm sure of it. We'll make tomorrow our fish day, since you two men are going to Tío's secret fishing spot tomorrow by the mangroves."

Paco's face brightened. "Oh bueno, I'm hungry! But let me play one more time!" He bent down to flick a marble of fire-engine red into one of traffic-light green.

"All right, mijo," said Tía Lourdes. "Your tío and I will get ready while you play one more time. But *cinco minutos*, little one, and not a second more! If you are still playing when we get in the truck, then it is straight to the washroom for you at the cafeteria. You will end up last in line behind the vaqueros. You might just have *papas* and charro beans to choose from after they have cleaned out the meat trays."

Tío and Tía entered the trailer, and Paco flicked the red marble. After it had struck the green and both had careened away, they gave place to a marble he had not seen before.

Who put that here? Was it Tío or Tía or someone else? It is not one of the six the raccoon gave me. And it is not the one I rescued from the dark water. I must see this new one.

He stretched out his hand and brought the new marble to his eyes. Before him was a world within a world. Bubbles hung like planets among milky streams of stars. Waves of creation poured over them toward a center both generous and unreachable, a place all things streamed to, and yet a place nothing could touch. And though every element of that world was complete and comprehensible when discerned individually, together they formed an everlasting dance that could not be traced.

Beside this new marble, Paco added the first one Patch had offered him, and to these two, the one Paco had rescued from the sea. He beheld all three. The first one carried an aquatic flame inside: green touching blue and blue touching green. The rescued one glowed gray-green with a hint of open sky. And the new one was beryl green with a hint of untilled earth. He touched the three and gently rolled them within his palm as one single mystery.

And as Paco sat entranced by the world within the marbles, the world around him faded. And in the fading, the boy whom the birds named Miracle became like a shadow of a great rock in a thirsty land. No visible change came upon the boy, and yet the change was undeniable.

—◊◊◊—

Plod gave a gentle neigh. "The air just changed. There's some sort of shade here now that's more than what the manplace gives. Nothing changed appearance, but the feel of where we're standing sure changed. It's like we're in a place no dust storm could reach. A solid shelter."

Patch lifted his head, attentive. "Yes, I sense it too! There's a refuge from hot winds here now. A *new* wind, or maybe 'breath' is a better word. I, I think they kinda mean the same thing anyway, don't they? A sort of special air that's, well, personal."

Bog hopped onto the edge of the water dish, perching there with his sticky pads as he tasted the atmosphere with his tongue. "I agree, friends. This is an air that is not from the Valley. It is mountain air from a fresh country. A tearless realm."

Patch brightened and poised as if to jump upon a prize. "It's a breeze from Eden, I bet!"

Just then, the quiet flicker of a shadow crossed over them. Chalice the Canada goose passed by, her swift silhouette imprinting beside the horse just beyond the rim of the canopy's mark on the ground. The friends turned to see her. She wheeled around toward them, giving the call of her kind, which prompted Paco to pause with the marbles. The goose landed.

"Hail to you, creatures of the Sixth Day! " said Chalice breathlessly.

"And hail to you, creature of the Fifth Day!" replied Bog. "We are already at peace, but your presence makes it richer."

Plod tapped a hoof. "Welcome, traveler. Rest your wings a spell and enjoy the shade. You're mighty welcome here."

Chalice waddled toward the basin where Bog kept watch. Instinctively, the Gulf Coast toad bloated his throat just in case the goose needed reminding that he was not on the bill of fare. But the goose gave a polite nod to the toad, making it clear that all she needed was relief from the heat of the journey. After taking a long drink, she dipped her head into the water, raised her beak, and let the water flow down her back. She shook her wings and christened the toad, who croaked in surprise.

Patch laughed. "She got your goose, ha ha!"

Bog smirked at the raccoon, annoyed at the joke but pleased with the pun.

Chalice turned to the boy. She approached and sat down next to him as he placed the marbles, now eight in all, in his pocket. "I'm glad to see the manchild Miracle looking so well. He was near death when I found him, but he has found mercy from you, his friends, and he has found mercy among the sons of Men."

Miracle understood Chalice to be speaking of him, for he saw how the goose looked at him.

"Yes!" he told her. "I am well! My friends were with me, so I was not alone, even when I was in the truck of Señor Gaston after he caught me at the hay bales. Even in the rusty place I was not alone, the place where the Tío Sergio and the bad men tried to take me. The birds with long legs helped me run from that place! The gate helped me too. But Papá Eli and Ubi helped most of all. Now I am safe! And look! New clothes! My new tío and tía—José and Lourdes—they gave them to me. They said I have grown. But Tía kept my old clothes. I saw her put them in a drawer. She told me, 'Mijo, I want to remember these days forever, and your clothes will remind me. They will tell me the story of how we found you. They will tell me the story of how our family began.'"

The goose bowed before the young prince, then lifted her head in wonder. "There is a great calm here. It is the same calm as the face of the lagoon in the morning when the water is so smooth the sky rests in it like a twin, and two suns appear instead of one."

"Yes," Bog said. "The peace here is like a river, and would that that river overflow its banks! Then there would be more than enough for frog and fly alike in this fallen world."

Chalice sighed. "We need such a river, oh Keeper of Odes, for the one which flows through the Valley has no such peace. I have just come from the Lady River. Behold, she is fainting! The great lady is fainting! No rain has fallen, and Man drinks her dry with no restraint and no remorse. I saw it from above! The sweet mouth of the lady slowly closes at the place called Boca Chica, where her waters kiss the sea. I saw a sight that caused my wings to drop: a sandbar just below the face of the tide. Closer and closer to the air it rises as the Lady River faints. And when she has altogether fainted the sandbar will become a *land*bar; a bridge between two manrealms where starfish are stranded and fish cannot swim. A seal upon the sleep of the Lady River."

Patch stood on his haunches, his ring tail rapidly tapping the ground. "This is bad news! What can be done?"

"I do not know," Chalice said. "We all wait for rain— Man, beast, and blade of grass alike. We all wait for mercy. We all are in the same Valley."

Patch clasped his paws and dropped his chin against them. "There must be something I can do!"

Bog hopped back into his water dish with a plop. "What, ask the sun to dim his rays? He sharpened them for us to help make hot tea for the manchild, but to cover his face over the whole Valley? Now that's a tall order. You'd have to ask our falcon friend to persuade him for a second favor."

Patch shook his head as he remained in a prayer-like pose. "Well, even if the sun did go ahead and do us the favor, it wouldn't help much. Living things can bear most any hot day as long as there's water to drink. I think I'll leave the sun to do its job. But what about if I do something to remind the sky of rain? Maybe *that's* within reach of my paw. I'm a small creature to be daring such a thing, I'll admit, but then again, if you really think about it, all of us, even the lord of the Valley, are small compared to the sky. We're all kinda equal before the big tent above us. I reckon that means we all have an equal chance at making something happen."

Patch tested the ground with his nose, for that is the raccoon way, even if the answer is beyond the sense of smell. After a moment he shot up with bright eyes and turned in the direction of the ranch cafeteria, whose screen door to the kitchen he knew well. He launched into a scamper.

"Where are you going?" Plod asked with a raised voice.

"I'm going on a Borrow and I'll see you late tomorrow," he said. Then he halted in a puff of dust as suddenly as he had scampered.

"Wait! Hey, now that's a good rhyme: 'I'm going on a Borrow and I'll see you late tomorrow.' I just stumbled on it like I do most good things. Maybe I'll become a songwriter like you one day, Bog!"

"Maybe!" Bog shouted back. "But you had better put that rhyme to song this very second! Poetic inspiration comes and goes like midnight whip-poor-wills. Make a nest for them while they pass before they go back into hiding."

Patch sat facing the friends but staring into space. "That word 'midnight' is useful," he whispered to himself. Then he raised his voice. "Okay…here goes!"

And, clearing his throat, he released his first poem:

I'll go on a Borrow till midnight tomorrow
With ebony boughs for a bridge
I'll search for a treasure, the moon taking pleasure
To watch how I open a fridge

I know of a winter that never a splinter
Of sunlight or summer can reach
A dish full of hailstones like ducks in a row
Or pelicans lined on a beach

They wait for a dropping in water or plopping
In drinks to the slaking of thirst
They cool off the drinker who's waiting for rain
Unless I can get to them first!

I'll pull out the frozen and pop out a dozen
Reminders of glaciers and snow
To chill the resaca and shiver the perch
I'll charm the June sky with a show

The air will discover and form up a cover
A canopy thick overhead
While wobbling ice cubes awash in the pond
Outdo the blank storm banks instead

What's this! Clouds awaken from sleep they are shaken
As jealousy racks them in pain
And floods them with fury to take up the charge
As thunderheads pour out their rain!

Patch took in a breath, body in the stance of a victor, but eyes marveling at what had just come out of his mouth.

Bog crooned in praise. "Bravo! Bravo, Patch of Palo Verde! A worthy first poem! A virtually flawless performance in the meter and rhyme of the traditional ballad!"

Patch bowed. "Thank you!"

Bog hopped out of the water dish with a flourish. "You show promise, oh Keeper of the Secrets, one for each ring on your tail."

Plod whinnied. "Sounds like you'll be adding a bit of variety to the program."

Bog looked at him askance. "Plod, if you knew a bit more about meter, you'd see quite a variety in my poetical works! And it's a *craft*, not a program, if you please."

Plod nipped at a fly, whapping it with his tail as it escaped his teeth. "I'll take your word for it. All I can say is that poems and their forms are like horses and their tackle. The occasion tells you the tackle, whether it's a buggy or bareback or barrels to race. Like when the wind blew at the dying pond. It was clear what I needed to harness up to, and the poem galloped in it."

"A good critique, my equine friend," Bog replied.

Chalice honked and flapped her wings toward Patch as he departed. "Well done, Treasure Keeper! You just found another treasure! May the wind be at your back as you go on your Borrow!"

"Thank you!" Patch replied over his shoulder. "I'll hide in the hollow of an ebony tree behind the manplace they call the 'chow house.' It has those dishes of hailstones I mentioned in my poem. They sit like cartons of eggs in boxes that hum and keep winter going year-round. Once night falls and Man has laid down his work for the day, my work begins. I'll borrow the hailstones, go to a resaca, and offer the sky a reminder of rain!"

—m—

While Patch bided his time in the ebony hollow behind the chow house, Tío José relaxed inside that house. He leaned back from his empty plate. So did Tía Lourdes and Paco.

"*¡Delicioso!*" exclaimed Tío José as he slapped his belly. "Raphael's cooks are the best! The key lime pie was a dream too."

"Sí," said Tía Lourdes, "almost as perfect as mine!"

And they all laughed.

"I see one more slice up there at the counter. I believe it has my name on it, *dulce dama*."

But as Tío José spied the slice, behind it, a man passed by.

Tío's face changed. He glanced at his wife, sober now, all the laughter of the former moment gone.

Tía Lourdes gave her husband a nod, speaking a wordless warning. Her husband responded in the affirmative. She turned to Paco.

"Mijo, let's go. I have groceries to shop for and new shoes for you too. You can't go about wearing what Tío bought you for wade fishing. Let's look for some decent sneakers, but we won't go until I have *personally* watched you brush your teeth at the trailer. When we come home after shopping, you can play marbles and sing stories to your four-footed friends, but when you do, don't go anywhere but their barn. I want you always in sight of Raphael's people."

"Yes, Tía."

And the two left.

The din of the cafeteria died down as the dust-covered ranch hands took final swigs of iced tea. The staff began cleaning the far end of the floor with Pine-Sol. The smell of the cleaner crept across the room, prompting vaqueros to rise as it reached each of them.

Tío José saw the man again. He walked among the vaqueros as they bused their plates. He did not chat with any of them, nor did any of them greet him. He wore an apron smudged with the red-brown of dried blood. A butcher's apron.

Sergio reached the table.

Tío José rose and stood silent before him.

"You look nervous," Sergio said, smiling. He pulled out an old bandanna, took off his glasses, and wiped the perspiration inside the lenses. "No need to be nervous; I am on the ranch clock. I do not do my other job until I am off it."

Tío José said nothing.

"But I do have some advice for you, José Benavides."

"What do you want?" said Tío José in a growl of a whisper. "Say your piece and be done with it."

Sergio delayed, savoring the discomfort. He smiled and spoke slowly.

"El Dragón craves the child. And he always gets what he craves. Do not become too attached to this little one. If you do, you will end up in the same boat with him, and you do not want that. No good meals where he is going."

He began to walk away. Then he paused after a few steps, straightening himself, touching the back of a chair one finger at a time until the whole hand grasped it. He turned toward Paco's guardian.

"We have to clean up the mess, amigo, clean it up together. Otherwise, no more barbecue for you to enjoy. Just an empty pit."

"*¡Piérdete!*" Tío José shouted.

Instantly, the cafeteria became silent. All looked at Tío. All turned to see the one he had commanded to get lost.

Sergio nodded respectfully and walked away while the vaqueros around him busied themselves wiping down tables already clean.

7

THE STAKES OF THE QUEST

After Oracle's encounter with Paladin the rhino, he came upon a levy crowned with Rio Grande ash trees, the kind of grove called a "motte" in the tongue of Man. It was the heat of the day. The cat of Sian Ka'an climbed into an ash where the branches converged to make a broad space, hammock-like, where he could recline without gripping the bark. He took in the unknown realm around him with eyes both sharp and docile, that kind of aloof vigilance only cats can do.

Just beyond the ash trees, he spied a stock tank where a family of nutria busied themselves. The sound of a congested water pump led him to search the bank until he found a pipe sticking into the air above the receding surface. Water spurted from it then quickly died away into trickles while the mechanism strained for more from its drought-stricken source to manage another spurt. The nutria swam by the pipe toward a new home they were building where the bank offered reeds both green and dry. They disappeared and reappeared at the mouth of their den, sometimes alone, sometimes minding their kits. The sun bore down upon their beaver-like backs and caused the sweaty oil thereof to shine like a slick of diesel, the film on their fur winking colors as it played with the light in the heat-soaked air.

There, in the Rio Grande ash, Oracle slept as the cicadas sang their throbbing litanies and the gulf breeze rocked the trees. That night, the jaguar stretched his limbs and hopped down. But when he attempted to greet the nutria as they swam in the moonlight, assuring them he preferred fish to fur, they fled more swiftly than the African grazers had, darting off without so much as a word or parting glance. And so, the Cat Who Remembers reclined by their den and fished for molly, leaving most of his catch at the mouth of their den. And at sunrise, the lord of the Valley continued on his way, exploring a bent but living world.

At midday, he came upon a great black willow tree overlooking a resaca deeper than the stock tank.

This body of water still has the depth to withstand these days of the brass sky without Man's intervention.

The jaguar scratched the bark of the black willow with a greeting. "Hail to you, oh Sentinel of the Waters, for the shelter you give while I drink. I am Oracle of Sian Ka'an, a realm ten moons away. I am known to the oldest cypress of the Valley, one who reaches the sky above the rest near the Lady River. I am known to a fallen cottonwood, whose trunk tore open a way for me to go free and swim the flowing path which Man blessed with the name Brazos. And I am known to the wild olive, the Lonely Tree, who is now lovely, for I have answered the prayer prayed among her branches seventy springs ago."

The willow stirred, her leaves moving like a curtain touched by a breeze. "Welcome to the manrealm of South Texas. Welcome, Sire Long Absent. Be at home in the Valley."

Oracle looked into the thick foliage above. "Oh Rooted One, though I have been in the Valley before, I have not been in this very place. Help me learn more about where I stand."

"I will, oh Royal One. To the north is a vast realm of cattle and mesquite. King Ranch is its name. To the southeast is a great refuge called Laguna Atascosa, one of the realms Man has set apart for wildlife. And beyond thick cityplaces farther south is the Lady River, whom you know, the one Man calls the Rio Grande, whose imperiled waters mark the limits of two nations. Many of my kind once stood on the banks of the Lady River—and many of your kind—all the way to river's end, where the wind-worn dunes meet the sea at a place called Boca Chica."

Oracle took in a slow, pensive breath. "Thank you. I too desire to run to river's end and the place you speak of." And he reclined to rest beneath the willow.

There was silence. Oracle let it flood in, ripe with unspoken words. Somewhere in the distance, a family of long-billed thrashers called to one another as a gulf breeze, making its regular blustery course from sea to land, blew through. The willow bowed and waved above the jaguar.

"Oh tree, in this second time in the Valley, I have met new kinds of creatures, wary and strange. They are not of Sian Ka'an as I am, but they are not of this realm either."

"Those would be the animals Man has placed here," said the willow. "I see them as they pass by, and the wrens and the hummingbirds tell me about them. They say they make great boasts even though they are newcomers from far away. Man has settled them here alongside us, the native trees and animals, for he hopes to steward all in one grand wilderness. It is a large land, and a four-footed one can make a three-day journey before finding the sharp wires of the ironthorn shaping it. The Man who is prince of this realm has named it Eden's Bend."

Oracle lifted his forepaws to the trunk, anchoring them there as he stretched his body tail-ward. "Ah, so I am in the manrealm Eden's Bend where I was before! This is where a great blue heron and an aplomado falcon told me that my friends abide. Oh you whose slender leaves host the feathered ones, have any of the birds spoken of a special band of animals: a raccoon who keeps borrowing, a horse who keeps plodding, and a toad who keeps the odes of his ancestors?"

The willow swayed in the wind. "I do not know of them. There are many who come and go on Eden's Bend as the prince of it busies himself securing his domain."

Oracle sat, considering the resaca and the variety of trees, shrubs, and grasses surrounding it. "'Eden's Bend.' The prince has named his realm after the first garden. Does this mean the manrealm is a refuge like the Laguna Atascosa you tell me about?"

"At times a refuge, at times a hunting ground," said the willow as a gust bent it leeward. "For the echo of the name of the first garden is not the only sound in the air here. Death is here too, as it is in all realms this side of Eden. For, as the wrens and hummingbirds tell me, though the prince of Eden's Bend has built a dwelling where he watches them at leisure, yet from time to time Man hunts the deer and their great-horned foreign cousins. And when the coyote or the cougar become too perfidious, Man hunts them too. You also may be hunted, for all I know."

"I see," said Oracle. "Man has gathered the animals here to rule them with his Three Choices."

"To rule them and to harvest them," said the tree as the wind ceased and she came to rest. "The prince of Eden's Bend raises animals to serve the desires of his tribe. Stout and ruddy cattle with names like Santa Cruz and Santa Gertrudis. But the prince has also placed great long-necked birds here with fierce feet and unfriendly beaks: the ostrich and the emu. These serve Man's desires too. Their flesh fills Man's hunger, their oil offers health, their hide a covering, and their feathers vainglory. And on the southern end of this realm the prince has built a great tower filled with fire from the heart of the earth, a tower ascending to the stars like a meteor seeking the home from which it fell. That is what the prince has done. It is his realm, and he rules it."

"So is the right of the prince," Oracle said, and he reclined while his tail moved in tandem with his meditations. "His right and his privilege. We animals were given to him so that he might make his choices over us, be our individual ends glorious or practical, miserable or memorable. For we all return to dust, but before we do, Man's choices rule us."

Oracle yawned and climbed to a willow branch overhanging the water. "If it pleases you, oh Friend of Green Shadows, I shall abide here until the sun sleeps and the moon sings. For I see our hearts freely share themselves, and one should not hurry from such a gift."

"Yes, sire, it pleases me too that you abide. Let us remain with one another till the sun goes down."

"Thank you. I will gather the grace that rest and fellowship bring before I put my paw forward again."

"Where will your paw go, oh Cat of Sian Ka'an?"

"My paw will risk the long arm of Man and his fire rods to find the path picking up where the last lord of the Valley left off. And once I find it, I will take it—take it until I find the shadow cat, that lost feline of the House of Herpailurus. I will take the path until I call a Council of the Cats. I will take the path until creation gathers again for a Court of the Animals as they did in the days of Kahoo, the last jaguar."

A moan rose among the branches. "Kahoo…no one has spoken that name among my branches for many a spring. And you have come to pick up his trail?"

"Yes, that is where I have put my paw forward, that Eden's air may abide for a time in the Valley's twilight days. I will impart the Breath of Remembrance, that a season of grace and honor may linger among the animals. Nevertheless, it is Man's choices marking off the path's edges. He can pour winter on springtime or convert it to an endless summer. It is up to him, for he wears the Crown of Three Choices."

"The lords of the animal kingdom like you and Kahoo rule within the circle of that triune crown. The trees are also subject to it."

"Yes, Man has dominion over where we place our paws and where you put down roots. He is our gatekeeper."

The willow groaned. "Alas, the gatekeeper has wandered far from the gate he was given to keep!"

"Yes," Oracle sighed. "Very far. But he remains our ruler. We must wait to see what he will do: return me to the bars of my capture, or leave me free to roam, or claim me through death as a prize of his dominion. For I am under him, as are you and all other living things of the Valley that breathe the air of this world."

The willow listened. Her trunk creaked from a desire deep beneath the bark. "No Council of the Cats has taken place for an age, and no Court of the Animals either."

"All the more reason I should summon them. For the Cats of the Three Tribes—the Three, as they were once called— will long outlast me, they and their offspring."

"That would be a new tree if you could plant it."

"I do intend to plant it, for though I have yet to meet any of the Three, it is clear from every creature that the Valley has fallen asleep. The animals have forgotten their names. Therefore, I know what I must do. I must awaken them. If I can restore the cats to humility before one another and courage before all, then I will have influenced this realm far beyond what my one paw could ever do. If I succeed, a time of peace and dignity will return in the Valley's twilight days this side of Eden. A last flourishing. A final spring."

The willow swayed, but from a motion in the inmost rings of her heart. "What if your planting fails to take root? What if there is no final spring?"

The burdened jaguar bowed his head. "Then the animals of the Valley will remain rootless wanderers until the dust and water hosting their spirits returns to the earth, and they are no more. That is the cost if the quest is lost."

The willow moved her branches as one stirring in a dream. "Better to be a seed-bearing tree than an ornamental one. You, oh Cat of the Long Journey, desire the fruit that remains. You desire to hold a Court of the Animals like Kahoo the Grave, the last jaguar, who drank the waters beneath my boughs and reclined among my roots. That is a noble thing, but even Kahoo did not achieve this."

Oracle dropped to the ground on all fours and stood at the foot of the tree. "Truly, he abided here?"

"Yes," the willow replied. "I recall his endeavors. Sensing he was in his last days, Kahoo convened the court three times in urgent effort to leave all in order before his demise, but he found no smooth path ahead for the Valley. For the animal kingdom had fallen into division and disarray due to wars between themselves and destruction at the hand of Man. Therefore, the last jaguar could barely persuade them to gather, let alone agree. Distress produced deaf ears, and deaf ears a scattering of the tribes."

"I believe you," Oracle lamented, "for tales not unlike yours creep ever closer to my own jungle realm in the Yucatán. But be that as it may, oh Well-Watered One, if I can give the Breath of Remembrance to whomever will receive it at the Court of the Animals, then no lord of the Valley need ever appear here again, for all in this realm would drink from the life-giving words flowing from the Days of First Things, when the Namer named us. Whatever Man may do to me in the hour of his decision, this is what I must complete before that hour comes."

The gulf breeze returned, and the willow moved with the invisible waves. "But what if Man permits you to roam? I have heard of such things. Among those who would seek to take you as a trophy there are also those who would seek to lengthen your time on earth. Yes, some would honor your life by permitting your breath to remain. Perhaps those kinds of Men, and not the other, will find you first and bring you to a preserved realm where you are free to roam. Perhaps it is even here, in this manrealm. Then you could mete out decisions just and fair for many springs, like the great Kahoo before you. For I perceive Eden in your breath, and my root revives at its presence. And my true name comes to me, the one Eve, the beloved of Adam, prophesied when she caressed my branches, which pour down like tears while green with hope: Charmolypi, joyful sorrow. Therefore, I know who you are. You are of the Ones Who Remember. You are of the Flock of the Lion. It would be a good thing for you to linger in the land."

Oracle bowed in honor to the tree. "You have spoken truly. That is who I am. And you have also spoken truly concerning Man. If he permitted me to roam, I could go here and there and intervene. I could make decisions just and fair for many springs as did Kahoo before me. But this, too, is a short-lived glory, something good, but bound by a sunset that must sooner or later come. However, if I give others what I have, that same breath which has awakened you to your true name, then the animals of the Valley need not track me down when in need, nor I them. If I give them what I have, they carry the path within them, the memory of Eden. And they can begin again whether my paw is present or not, for they will remember their names. New beginnings always start with a memory, and Eden's memory is at the root of their creation."

The tree rocked in the wind. "You describe a mature seed. You would that the root in you become the root in them. Then they can flourish for a time and not merely survive. Then they can be like trees with branches heavy with the good fruit they carry. Yes, oh Cat Who Remembers, that is a good seed to plant. Better to bear fruit and risk a shorter reign than to prove your strength and rule long."

"Yes. If I poured all my strength into proving my reign, I could be strong indeed for a time. But what good would that do? I would have my way for a day, then die. And with me would die all the seeds I could have sown in the soil of others. Better to give my life away than to live my life *my* way."

Silence descended again, placing itself like a gentle mantle upon the hearts of the jaguar and the willow. A family of clay-colored thrushes called to one another as a breeze blew through, and the slender leaves of the tree whispered a song as they brushed one another. Oracle curled his body within the niche of two roots radiating from the willow like motherly arms. There he abided with the tree until the sun had set. Then he rose and continued his journey.

8

THE CHOICE OF THE GREEN JAY

In the second watch of the night, Oracle entered a thicket of young palo verde trees. Their slender branches and needle-thin leaves received the glow of the round and rising moon, as did the grass beneath them. Alive with heaven's glow, the grass met the feet of the one who trod upon it with a hushed reverence.

Ahead of the jaguar, on the lowest branch of a palo verde, perched Gem the green jay. The night muted the banner of her colors, which in sunlight were the unmistakable signature of her tribe: a vivid green body; a florid blue crest framed in bold, black trim; and a bright yellow breast dusted with emerald.

Gem had awakened and was preening herself in preparation for a night watch, for the thrushes and thrashers had spread a rumor of a new animal they had seen, and the green jays had reached a swift consensus that they would not be caught unawares.

Normally, her preening was preparation for the pre-dawn liturgy belonging to her tribe. It was their custom to sing while the animals of the day made half-awake whispers to rouse the others and those of the night gave last-minute signals of their departure. Such was the green jays' regular ritual.

But here, outside their routine in the night's second watch, Gem sensed the movement of something new.

A sphere of strange air moves ahead of it. Dense and light at the same time. No sight of it yet.

Gem went on preening, but more slowly, with longer pauses to listen. Then, in mid-preen, with her beak between body and wing, she knew that the "something" had arrived just below her branch. She opened her left eye and looked down.

A king was there, a ruler in a royal coat: a member of the House of Panthera Onca from the Yucatán.

Without conscious thought, her head came out from under her wing. She stared at the New Thing, who had paused beneath her branch. He stood with eyes forward but head low, patiently surveying where he was.

His manner communicates depth, not caution. He lives in the moment he finds himself—and rules it.

She smelled his warmth wafting up to her, the air of one greater than herself and more dangerous.

Gem froze, for the sight of a six-foot-long jaguar evoked every last fiber of fear that had been passed down to her from her primordial "fore-feathers," as the gregarious jays deliberately called them. The very quills of her skin screamed to move her beak with the alarm cry of her tribe, a sound similar to a rattling bell on a wind-up clock, the call that would rally a mob of fellow green jays to cloud about the predator, shouting, swooping, and finally compelling the confused invader to withdraw. Her mouth was open, a vapor away from sounding the alarm.

But she chose not to. She remained perfectly still. For moonlight covered the cat's golden coat in soft silver and transformed the white trim of his fur into ethereal ermine. Moonglow rested on his eyes and anointed his fur, even the fullness of his whiskers, which radiated from his face in slender, crystalline lines.

Oracle put one paw forward, setting it upon the ground as calmly as if it rested upon an imperial orb, gentle yet solid. The patterns of his coat were an epic poem. His spots in rosette tapestry seemed all movement and dignity and strength at the same time. The choreography of the spots dazzled Gem's gaze, for while she fixed her eyes on one point, the spots flowed toward that point as if drawn into an invisible portal, swirling about it before disappearing. And yet the spots never exhausted themselves but were ever resupplied from the periphery of her vision. Joy and dread danced with one another as she beheld the cosmos of spots.

Before she knew it, Gem was not even looking at the jaguar anymore, although of course she was quite fixed on him. She was looking at the beauty of the thing, which is far more lovely than the thing itself and far more powerful. That beauty reached back in time and disarmed her primeval alarm.

She spoke. "You…you…It's *you*…Who are you? Who are you, oh Cat of the Southern Jungle?"

He looked up and saw her. "I am Oracle of Sian Ka'an, the lord of the Valley."

"How did you get here?"

"Man set me free."

"Man?" asked Gem, with the unusual liberty of speech that comes when one is shaken. "Man set you free? Man is meant to dominate, not liberate, is he not?"

"I think your word is correct on both counts, Green One, for Man has power to do both, and he chooses whichever he wills. He is a creature of the Sixth Day, not the Fifth Day like you. His choices govern yours. And the choice of the Seventh Day governs his."

"So, Man *chose* to set you free?"

"Yes. And now my own choices begin."

Oracle considered Gem. "You remind me of a tribe whose feathers brighten the bushes of my Sian Ka'an home. They are called the Yucatán jays of the House of Cyanocorax."

"Oh, yes!" Gem replied. "They are cousins of us greens! We are also of the House of Cyanocorax, and our tribe extends from southwest of where the Yucatán jays dwell to here in the Valley. We're green, of course, but they're black with blue wings. As for us, our blue is on our heads with a black bib. We've got some yellow feathers, but *their* yellow is on their beaks, on their legs, and 'round their eyes. They don't let up for a minute in their chatter, but we greens have a wider repertoire *and* a sweeter song, if I do say so myself."

Oracle grinned. He sat and curled his tail back and forth around his body. "Then it is good that I have met you, for your family ties to my birthplace inspire trust. I would like to confirm with you what I have heard already through the testimony of the trees: the allthorn three moons' journey into Mexico, the cypress I abided with on my second morning in the Valley, and the willow I spoke with today. All have guided me well, but an additional confirming witness is not a bad thing while I am learning my way around new territory this second time in the Valley, especially when the new witness is not a plant, with no vested interest in old wood. So, tell me of this place. Where am I, and what lies to the south? For I sense that southward is where I should go."

Gem tapped her tail on the palo verde. "This is the realm of the Great River—or once great, really. The Lady has seen better days. It is the realm of the sabal palms, although only remnants remain. This is the realm of the bobcat and the ocelot, who rule as stewards in your absence. And this is the realm of Man, who dominates or liberates, just as you said."

Oracle reclined, his tail continuing to stir. "How can I reach the Great River? Ten moons ago, and two blue moons besides, I crossed it from the south. I kissed the Lady River, the keeper of the waters. I desire to see her again."

Gem stooped and opened her wings in a tense posture. "The way is perilous, sire. It is broken up with ribbons of tar and stone, where Death overruns many. A thick jungle of manplaces lies between here and the Lady River, and Man fights to keep his places tame. Thus, the tame places are often dangerous for you, while the wild places are safe only when Man is not hunting there. A few of Man create places to welcome wild ones like you, but many fight to keep your kind out. Many will not welcome you, because to welcome you would mean Man would no longer grasp the whole land with his hand, and the whole land is what Man wars to have until he alone is lord. That is why we green jays call him the Tribe of the Alone Ones."

The jaguar lowered his head in sorrow, but when he lifted it again his eyes were clear. "Tell me about the ocelots, oh cousin of the Inca jay, and tell me of the bobcats. How does the animal kingdom fare?"

Gem fluttered to the ground beyond the swipe of paws. "It fares poorly, sire. My fellow green jays tell me the lead bobcat and ocelot spend more time arguing than stewarding. The name of the ocelot is Pace and the bobcat's name is Force. But they are 'more rivals than rulers,' as my flock says. We cry this proverb when we swoop over them at the place where they take counsel, the place called Swog's Wallow. We green jays can be audacious, as I'm sure you've seen with my Inca jay cousins in the Southern Jungle. It is the way of the jay to call things as they are. The stewards growl back at us that they 'manage,' but we green jays—when we're clear of their claws, of course—retort that 'to manage' and 'to muddle' mean the same thing. Meanwhile the Valley languishes. No mystery remains in the ways of the animal kingdom. No sense of awe.

No hope. The nest has fallen, and the eggs are dashed. We are scattered twigs.

We have our tales, but we have no vision
We have our words, but we have no wonder
We have our stories, but we have no calling
We have our feathers, but we have no wings

The lord of the Valley let the song of the green jay flow through him like a brook among smooth stones. "Then it is right I have returned. It is good to be here."

Gem hopped forward. "Yes, I see it is, sire, but not all the animals will think so, and not all of Man. He will hunt for you."

Oracle lifted his face heavenward. "See how the evening star sinks in the western sky. She confirms your word that my time is short. But the limit is good, for it compels me to choose. If I only have time to do what is most important, then the path ahead is clear. I know what I shall do."

The green jay ventured one hop closer. "What, sire?"

"I shall summon the cats in council; then I shall summon the animal kingdom. I shall hold court at the Sanctuary of Sabal Palms. I shall call each one back to his beginning place, the memory of the Days of First Things."

"Oh, that it would be!" sang Gem.

"And I shall summon Man. I shall summon the Tribe of the Alone Ones. I shall meet with him at river's end and give him the choice of what to do with me, for that is justice. To him belongs the Crown of Three Choices: to kill, to capture, or to let me remain free. I was formed for Man; he named me. But I shall come to him as myself and not as another. I shall come to him as a jaguar. If I live, I shall live like one, and if I die, I shall die like one. Whether I live or die, I shall do it well and do it fully."

In the silence, Gem mused on the Oracle's words. *He whispers not only to me but to all of the Valley, both Man and beast. It's too weighty for me to fully understand but too important to ignore. I must herald the news of the arrival of the lord of the Valley. I must proclaim it! Oh, the joy and fear are too great to contain!*

Gem came within a whisker length of the jaguar's face. Her legs trembled, her feathers too. "May I have permission to spread the news of your plan?"

Oracle looked into her face with a warmth that transferred as his breath touched her. She no longer shook as she breathed in Eden's air.

"Yes," Oracle said, "and as you do, make your way to the heads of the House of Lynx Rufus and the House of Pardalis, for the bobcats and ocelots are the stewards of the Valley in my absence, and therefore, I shall honor them. Tell Pace and Force I shall meet them at the place of their choosing for a Council of the Cats."

Gem bade Oracle farewell, made a figure eight before the moon, and flew off in eager haste to inform the stewards. Along the way, she gave this message to any who would listen:

"The lord of the Valley has returned and shall hold court again! He shall gather with you at the Sanctuary of Sabal Palms! The stewards of the Valley will go ahead of us. Be ready for the news!"

Gem was surprised by the responses of the animals, whose reactions generally fell into one of three categories. Some, like the nutria, a rodent not native to the Valley, lashed out at her with jeers and cynicism. Others—the whistling ducks, in particular—responded with wonder and elation. (*And you would think that they would have every reason to flee in dread and commotion*, thought Gem.) Others were overcome with perplexity and met in hurried consultations, almost ignoring Gem altogether.

Such was the case of the armadillos, who could not decide if this was good news, or bad news, or news of no concern, or if the jaguar's return might reduce the termite population or compel the fire ants to make an exodus for Mexico. A host of questions were muttered from mouths simultaneously, and the quick-beaked green jay tried her best to answer each one as fast as she could, flitting branch to branch above them. But alas, the poor eyesight and dull hearing of the armadillos made her chirping answers difficult to understand, and, in fact, created a flurry of follow-up questions. Often the questions included the words *implications* or *relevance* and led into almost every direction of thought.

What a dust devil they've kicked up! Gem thought. *It's as if they've forgotten my original message and are asking questions about long-standing debates of their own.*

Whatever the truth as to the source of their questions, no number of answers satisfied the armadillos but seemed to agitate them further, until they began barking questions into the air with words unfamiliar to Gem, such as *epistemology* and *hermeneutics*.

Gem fluttered faster. *I can't tell if they're directing their questions at me, or one another, or someone in their own imaginations!*

Frustrated with their "incompetent" green jay emissary, the armadillos eventually ignored her altogether and clustered in circles among themselves, each group selecting the armadillo with the thickest armor (implying wisdom and experience) to moderate (not to *lead*, mind you) a discussion as to how the armadillos should respond to this so-called Oracle.

9

A Light on the Water

The same moon watching the green jay's figure eight in the air beheld the raccoon's zigzag on the ground, for while Gem carried a trove of good news, Patch carried a tray of ice cubes. This was no small feat for the raccoon, who experimented with several methods of transporting the tray. He tried dragging it with his paws. He tried pulling it with his teeth. He tried tucking it under one foreleg. For a moment he even attempted to balance it on his head, steadying it with one limb while he hobbled on three. None of these methods was particularly elegant or efficient, but the combined effort of all the clumsiness was a slow, progressive, forward path. He reached the nearest resaca his nose could find.

Patch searched the banks until he found the hardest thing there, a dwarf plywood shed housing a water pump, from which protruded an algae-slathered PVC pipe sinking into the water. Grasping the ice tray with both paws, he turned it upside down and swung it with a bang against the side of the shed. Out dropped half the cubes. The rest fell free with two more taps of the tray. Gathering a few at a time, Patch plopped them in the water until all bobbed like fishermen's corks in the moonlight.

He lifted his head. "All right, you heavens! I've done what I can! Tell the sleepy sky that the hail I've just thrown in is pulling its weight to cool this drought-stricken pond, and no

85

thanks to the lazy clouds! It happened without them, thunderhead free! Who knows if this is the start of something new, where storm banks and downpours need not bother to display their glory! Let the Texas summer hear what a raccoon accomplished: he outdid the sky! Suit yourself if you're content with that arrangement, you deaf clouds, though of course your honor falls when a furry bandit steals your thunder! Yep, you stars and moon, pass that gossip on. I doubt the clouds will listen, but there's always a chance. Remember what our famed forefather Graynail the Southpaw used to say, 'One small seed can grow a forest!' He lived in Lost Maples State Park, where every single tree proves his proverb true!"

And with that, Patch breathed a sigh of satisfaction. "Well, I've done my part."

Exhausted from his Borrow, he reclined for a while. Then Patch dipped his paws into the pond and washed his face with them, the drops returning from his muzzle to the surface like drops of rain preceding a shower.

Patch frowned as he did his chore. "It's good to wash before I fish, but likely the sound of those drops drives off my dinner. Crabs and crawfish don't linger where whiskers are!"

Nevertheless, Patch lingered in the washing, for the water on his face gave off its coolness, and the coolness refreshed him from the heat of the day and the labor of the night.

The moon kissed the water with her round reflection. Patch saw her mirrored face.

"You have seen the whole tale. You sure take a long time to say anything, but when you do, it's sweet to hear. I reckon it takes time for you to drink it all in and turn it into sweetness. Like bees and their honey, I suppose. Slow in coming, but worth the wait and the risk of stings."

As he looked at her on the resaca's surface, another reflection caught his eye.

Patch squinted and craned his neck. "That couldn't be you too, could it? Can you give two reflections in the same water? Of course not. For then you wouldn't be true to yourself. You have only one face to give, not two."

Patch moved his tail methodically as he examined the second light. "Your color is not the moon's, more like a glow from a fire. Oh! You aren't a reflection at all, but a light of your own! You're a lamp floating on the water."

Patch stretched his neck and squinted his eyes. The lantern hosted movement.

"The light inside is *moving*. I must see this."

And in Patch splashed. There was no fear, for curiosity is an armor to fear, much as focus is an armor to fear and many another foe who threaten to steal the treasure we seek.

With each stroke of the paw, the lantern loomed slightly larger, and the movement therein—the dance of the light—disclosed itself to be not the light of a lone flame but a gathering of flame-bearing creatures.

"Fireflies! It's a jar where Man has gathered fireflies! But why is it afloat here? Why adrift with no keeper? The fireflies can't open the lid, and after a while the jar won't be home to anyone. The light will go out, and dust will remain."

And now a better thing than curiosity overtook Patch: wonder. For if curiosity can set one free of fear, wonder can set one free to savor the moment. And savor he did.

There they were, a dozen fireflies aglow with the joy they carried within them, some hovering, some moving back and forth on the smooth surface of the glass as it slowly rotated. The light filled Patch's eyes and cast a luminous sphere around the jar. Patch's presence sent ripples that made the jar wobble the closer he came.

"You have caused quite a story for the folk of the pond, but that can't be the final thing you're known for. You were meant to fly. You were meant to give your glow to this jar only for a moment before moving on. And move on you must, if I can help."

The task turned out to be more difficult than Patch had expected. For one thing, he had to manage the basic task of remaining afloat ("I'm no good to you drowned!"). For another, the glass jar—of mason type with the kind of lid that seals preserves—offered very little in the way of something for him to grab on to. Its smooth sides proved hard to grasp, and its round shape seemed to always drive the jar away from his paws as he touched it. And yet Patch persisted, for the glow of the fireflies testified of life.

"A life that's sealed must be revealed!" Patch said.

At midnight, Oracle discerned the scent of a resaca as he passed through the branchy curtain of a eucalyptus grove. The water lingered in the air around them and then grew stronger as he entered the low-hanging leaves of a willow. It was there, as he passed through those leaves, that he heard the sound of water.

"This is not the sound of swimming, for it does not come and go in rhythm. This is the sound of wrestling, for the water splashes and trickles in constant motion. Who could be at work like this when the moon is bright and the still air carries every sound? Whoever he is, he is too preoccupied with his labor to worry about being found. Could it be the same one whose voice I heard shouting in the distance a while ago?"

Oracle emerged from willow at the resaca's edge, where a row of horsemint clumps, pagoda shaped, afforded him a parapet of sorts from which to look yet remain unseen. There, as the bergamot aroma of the horsemint bathed him, he perceived a glow on the water. A soaked and furry creature was at work upon that glow. The light drew the silhouette of its servant.

"You look familiar, oh Lamp Keeper," Oracle whispered. He descended into the water. Paw, limb, and body, he sank into the dark water and glided, motions unseen. He smiled.

—⊶—

Patch, meanwhile, had finally managed to loop his tail around the jar while grabbing the tip of it.

"Now if I can just sidestroke with one paw and tow you, we'll be on dry land soon."

As he turned, his eyes saw motion upon the dark waters. He let go, the jar just behind him, treading water between the fireflies and the mysterious movement before him.

"A beast of prey! Well, this is not how I thought I'd finish, but here we are. No one gets their dream ending, I suppose. One part misery and one part courage are all we're guaranteed, I guess. A gator will get nothing from that jar in his belly but a stomachache. Maybe I can give him a good hard toothache on my own way down that keeps him from trying out the fireflies until some other help for them comes along."

A voice called to him. "What makes you think I wouldn't help you with the fireflies?"

"Wha—? That sounds like—? Or—Oracle? Is that you? But you—you—you are in the north! Man took you away!"

"And Man sent me back. Everything had to bend to Kahoo's prayer, and it came about in a way that nothing but friendship could have fashioned."

"You're back! Oracle, you're back!"

And Patch thrashed his limbs in a hearty swim until he and his friend were rejoicing in a watery roll with splashes that sang with laughter—a half hug, half scramble that only the seriousness of brotherly love could have made possible. For after the joy of words comes the joy of abiding. And after the roll and the laughter, abide they did, floating before one another aglow with delight and aglow with the dance of the fireflies, who knew at once from the joy that shone before them that all would soon be well.

Together they ferried the jar to the shoreline, where Patch was able to sufficiently grasp the glass. He carried it to the parapet of horsemint. There, Oracle lay on his side and opened his mouth, wherein Patch placed the jar as one would place an item in a carpenter's vise. The jar was perfectly fixed in one position, for Oracle employed through his jaws just enough strength to accomplish that purpose—what the tribe of the Ones Who Remember calls gentleness.

Patch, alive with confidence and the comfort of his friend, did not fear to draw near. Then the one whom the Powhatan mantribe calls He Who Scratches with His Hands grasped the tightly sealed lid and turned it in counterforce to the fixed state of the jar in the jaws just beneath him.

The lid opened. Patch removed the flat sealing disc beneath it. The fireflies flew out like a sudden breeze from another world. But they did not flee. They lingered in a cloud and danced a slow, humble dance around the raccoon and the jaguar.

Now, fireflies are not known for their elegance nor their graceful flight patterns, but they are slow-flying servants who remember every act of wonder they have ever been a part of. From the long, openhearted conversations of Man on the back porch in the middle of the night, to the soldier in the trench for whom the dawn of the next day might be the doom of his last day, from lovers to lyricists to watchmen on the wall—the fireflies remember it all, not with words but with a dance retelling each tale.

Therefore, the fireflies, overjoyed at their release, compressed their clumsy choreography into a cloud so close to the friends that the bugs brushed their whiskers as they passed. And Oracle and Patch both knew—through the dance—the fireflies were telling them the story of how they had come to be in the jar in the first place, and of the series of tragic events that had led to their unwitting abandonment. They could even see by the patterns of light that these things were not held against those who had done them, for the tragedy had turned out to be a comedy that only the captive fireflies were privileged to have witnessed. Then they expanded their dance to long, happy arcs and dispersed one by one into the free air they were designed for, their distant farewells flashing like glimpses of shooting stars.

"You must meet my friends, the ones who helped me with the errand! The manchild Miracle is nearby too! There is much to tell, and even more to ask. But all in all, the sweet fruit has overtaken the sour, and a smile for every tear, I reckon. I 'carried the knot I couldn't untie' like you told me to, and goodness, did the threads lead to tangles and treasures! But come, meet my friends! They're this way!"

Patch ran as straight a path as he could, hopping fallen branches and dodging clumps of yaupon. Oracle followed, loping at a pace subordinate to his guide. Out of a thicket, they emerged to find bands of freshly turned earth and new fences. Patch plunged under one in the scrape he had made there, a trench that gave him seamless passage; Oracle followed, though with some difficulty and digging of his own, for a scrape that is deep to a raccoon is shallow to a jaguar.

As Patch watched Oracle emerge from the scrape, he gasped.

"Sire, your leg! What a gash! Such a terrible wound! What happened? Are you all right?"

Oracle shook the dirt off his fur. "More than all right, friend, for the wound worked wisdom in me."

"That scar is quite a price to pay for wisdom!"

"There is no other way this side of Eden."

"What happened?"

"A cousin pierced me."

"Ouch! It's one thing to have a stranger hurt you, quite another when it's kin. Did you trespass on his territory? Is that why? Certainly, he wouldn't have gone after you if he had remembered his name!"

Oracle shook loose debris out each paw. "We were both sojourners in a land a Man had set apart for himself and the wilderness. It was neither my cousin's territory nor mine. The law of pilgrimage should have disarmed our combat, but my cousin had become a law to himself. And you are right about what might have been had he remembered his name, but my cousin preferred what he already knew over discovering what he had forgotten."

"Wow, his preference caused you quite a pound of pain."

"And it caused me to be here with you too."

Patch drew near. "What do you mean?"

Oracle reclined before him. "The Man known as Brazos Ben, the ruler of a river realm, where he let the wild things grow and graze—he nursed me back to health with a mixture of medicines from the earth and from plants bearing cures in their crushing. Once I was well, he lifted me onto a manma-chine with steel wings that carried me here. And behold, in so doing, he served Kahoo's prayer! I arrived 'from the north and from the sky'!"

Patch marveled, thumping his tail. "Amazing! And you never planned it that way! It's like when I go diving into empty dens to escape the hunter and find shiny treasures in the dark, even a marble now and then! I dive in because of trouble, but I come out the richer because I find a gift stashed away, placed there by who knows who ahead of my diving in. My paws can't take the credit for the treasure, but the trouble can. Yep, it's the trouble that drove me to the treasure!"

"Yes!" Oracle replied. "So it is. Trouble can lead to treasure! Therefore, it is true to say that my three greatest troubles since I put my paw forward—the capture by Man, the torment of the grackles, and the fang of the cougar—served Kahoo's word in ways I never could have devised. The three great troubles did not even know the last jaguar's word! It had never entered their ears, and yet, like a creek in a flash flood, all their passion poured downstream in one direction, the direction I needed to go! They sent pain and delay, those three troubles, pain and delay as *servants* who brought me news of the path and the promises planted there. I could not have discovered the path and the promises on my own. I could not have found the treasure apart from the troubles that served me."

The two friends rose and continued on their way. But Patch, heart enlivened by the conversation, carried fresh thoughts about his treasure pouch, which he had hidden in the hollow of a eucalyptus ten moons ago, and two blue moons besides, when he set out on his journey with Oracle and the manchild Miracle.

I wonder if it's still there. I wonder if I'll ever see my treasures again. I would like to see them. I sure hope it doesn't take troubles to get me back there like it took for Oracle to get back here. Maybe there's another way, a shortcut 'round hardship. I sure hope so. I don't take a shine to troubles. Try to avoid 'em if I can. But there is the Breath of Eden now, that breeze with a mind of its own. Hard to predict but always on the move. Things sure are different with it. Maybe the troubles will be different too. A better sort of different.

10

PLOD AND BOG MEET ORACLE

Patch and Oracle coursed their way past sleeping field machines toward a sturdy new stable where an old horse swished his tail, looking out his stall window upon the stars while the other horses slept.

Plod heard feet approaching. His eyes grew wide.

"Bog, Patch brought a friend."

The toad climbed Plod and reached the place between his ears. He saw the huge silhouette of Patch's friend, a form made all the larger by the smallness of his escort.

Bog grabbed Plod's ear and whispered into it. "We'd best meet them in the corral, come what may. If they enter here, that friend of Patch will cause quite a commotion with your fellow horse folk. Whatever that shadow brute is, it will raise enough ruckus to bring every last gaucho to our door!"

Plod wheeled around and dropped his head over the stall gate, a kind called a "gossip gate" in the tongue of Man, for it dipped in the middle, affording the horses a means of seeing one another and trading tales. The gate was made of well-crafted oak and bore an iron latch.

"How do you suppose we can open this?" Plod asked. Bog hopped onto the latch and studied it. The iron, well forged with a touch of filigree, formed a loop like a wave in rip curl, which touched upon the latch proper where it pivoted on a bolt. To open it, a human hand had to pull the loop up such that the latch dropped from its catchment.

"If only this latch were the other way around," Bog said. "Then I could hop down on the loop and lift the long part away from its place like a seesaw. But I'm gonna have to push it up so the long part goes down, and that'll be a challenge. I think I'm up for it, though. Being around Patch has benefited my skills. It's that air about him…Plod, allow me to hold on to your nostril and lower me just below the loop. I've gotta get under it."

Plod gave a low neigh. "What if I sneeze?"

"Don't even *think* about sneezing! You'll launch me to kingdom come like that flying tower we saw!"

Plod tossed his head. "Well, there's no guarantees. Your pads tickle like a horsefly. It's all I can do to hold my breath."

Bog protested with a quiet croak. "No time for banter. I'm going down on that nostril of yours. Be brave! Hold back any blast reeling your bones. But if you do sneeze and I never return, make a good song of it!"

The horse scrunched his eyes tight and summoned his nose to hold back while the Gulf Coast toad clung to his nostril until he was just below the loop. Bog put his forehead on the iron and positioned his hind legs to power lift upward.

"I've got it! Hold still!"

Plod did so, Bog lifted the latch, and the gate swung open. The toad threw himself up the side of Plod's jaw and into his mane while the horse snorted repeatedly. They reached the corral just as their visitors did, who entered under the lowest of the three bars traversing the fence posts just as Miracle had done on the day the ostriches had brought him.

Patch beamed with joy. He rose on his haunches, placed a paw on his heart, and bowed. "Plod and Bog, may I introduce you to my very good friend who prefers fish to fur, the lord of the Valley, Oracle of Sian Ka'an."

And now Plod had his first true challenge with the "something new" Patch had described to him the first time they had met that warm summer night in the dilapidated stable not far from where he stood. At that time, the promise of Man's sweet elixirs had been enough to tolerate the unknown nature of the one who had sent Patch on his errand. But now, here before him was a great cat with the strength to spring farther than a horse with a saddle-worn back could flee.

Plod threw back his ears. "So, you're the new thing. I see now why Patch kept the picture cloudy. Tell me, partner, with all due respect, do new things eat horses?"

"New things make friends," Oracle said.

"Friends with grass-eaters?"

"Friends with friends."

"Am I a friend?"

"The raccoon needed you, and you helped him. A horse who does that does something friends do. And though it's only fair for friends to expect a benefit from each other, the fact remains that you went on no easy journey. You counted your life as something too unique to preserve in a stall and too common to do anything with other than give away. Yes, oh Homespun Servant of the House of Equus, I call that being a friend."

"Thank you," Plod said, and he bowed. Oracle saw the toad in the horse's mane.

"And who is your guide through the roads less traveled, I presume?"

The Gulf Coast toad hesitated to leave Plod's hair, for there above him was the great face of the new "lord of the Valley," as the Lady River had called him: legs like columns, body like the canvas of a champion's tent on the battlefield. Face fierce with authority and jaws that could swiftly devour him.

Looks as if my lifelong aspiration for a glorious ending is before me, but I can't even swallow, let alone croak a boast! These quivering legs of mine won't do me no good either. Whaddya know: here at the threshold of my dream come true, there ain't no glory at all! At least the kind of glory I was dreaming about. Just a knowledge that I'm a vapor and I've done my part. But if I've done my part with all my heart, well, that's glory enough.

Bog noticed among the jaguar's rosette spots a pattern resembling the lily pads of his home pond. He found strength again, for there is no strength like remembering who you are and where you come from.

It's a strength as unique as each one's own story is unique, I suppose, like a fragile snowflake and a fiery star that are one and the same.

Bog cleared his throat and looked straight into the eyes of the lord of the Valley.

"Patch," he said while he beheld the jaguar, "I ask your forgiveness for suspecting you of being full of foolishness. You were not foolhardy, friend. You were wholehearted."

The toad hopped off Plod's mane and croaked a long and solemn tone. "Hail, Chief of All Ponds. Hail, Wanderer from the Wetlands beyond the Wild Rim of the River. On behalf of my fellow keepers of the night watch, the House of Bufo greets you."

"And hail to you, Keeper of Odes. You remember the tales of your tribe, and now you, too, will be remembered in them."

"But sire, why should I be remembered? I have only done what all toads do. We have a tough hide, you know, and we throw that hide into tough places. It is our way."

"There are two kinds of courage," Oracle said. "One comes from having a tough hide. The other comes from having a new heart. Somewhere along the way, on one of those less-traveled roads you showed your friends, you found a new heart. That shall be remembered."

Bog crooned in gratitude and gave credit in song to many an ancestor whose story had been a prologue to his own.

The friends rested while Bog continued to sing. Comforted, they closed their eyes. The odes of the toad accompanied the deep interlude of the night's fourth watch. Then the dawn's first faint fingers stretched across the night sky to touch the moon in the southwest, caressing the lunar sphere like a precious marble late discovered. Bog put his songs to rest.

The raccoon sat up. "Oracle, like I said at Firefly Lake, Miracle is not far from here. He lives in the manplace of a kind aunt and uncle. Their hair is the color of winter, but their hearts are summer-warm. They let the boy spend as much time with us as he pleases. I'll go bring him to you."

Oracle stretched and stood. "Yes, Patch, that would be very good. When the aplomado falcon visited me as I journeyed on the Brazos, he told me of the deep grief and deeper mercy that had come upon the manchild. He told me his parents had departed for the Far Country, but the aunt and uncle have become like family to him—and so have you. It was in my heart to ask you about Miracle, but you knew my heart before I spoke it."

Patch twitched his tail. "That's because we're of the same heart, I reckon. When you go through a lot together, the path becomes the same even if the paw prints differ."

"Ah, well put," replied the jaguar meditatively.

A calm followed as each reclined in a togetherness so rich no new words were needed for a while, only a reflection on the words already known. There came a moment when each breathed deeply, as if they had just listened to a lovely song. Patch spoke.

"Oracle, the early morning light reminds me of the help the sun gave us to bring back the boy from Death's door with a brew of tea from the plants of the healers. Miracle will be awake soon."

The Cat Who Remembers paced the edge of the corral. "Then we shall soon see him, and more than just see. My heart tells me Miracle has a part to play in my search for a lost tribe called the jaguarundi. While marooned in a manplace of gates and gardens, a great striped cousin told me that the jaguarundi—also called the 'shadow cat'—still lives. He has not perished, but is hidden. And if he remains hidden until the final sunset on this realm, then the Valley shall never know the fullness of the final spring reserved for its last days. I have clues of where to find him, but I foresee that Miracle will be a part of their finding, for being a child of Man, he bears the image of the Maker. He is our gatekeeper, not we ourselves. The honor of revealing hidden things is bound up in the authority of the Namer."

Bog hopped into the corral's water trough and out again, dripping with the refreshment of the plunge. "It is good that the manchild is useful."

Oracle gave a gentle growl. "Useful, yes, but that is not the root of the matter. Here is the root: that he simply *is* and that he bears the image of the One who made us. Yes, that is the root. His usefulness is a slender branch. Even if that branch were removed, the root would remain. And the root is the heart of the tree. We do not choose our friends for their branches but for their roots. We had best choose our friends *before* we discover them to be useful, not *because* they are useful."

"I see," said Bog. "Like finding a lost tribe we belong to, no matter our rank or role or if we're the runt of the litter."

"Yes, oh Poet of the Pond. This child is of our tribe, whether lost or found, whether ill or sound. All the rest, including his usefulness, is a second gift resting upon that first, like raindrops resting on the golden blossoms of the peacock trees in my native realm. And as with the child, so with the jaguarundi. When the one helps us find the other, the greatest gift they both will give is not what they do for us but who they *are* to us. Such treasures are worth unearthing. When our friend named Miracle comes to visit, we shall behold that treasure."

The jaguar departed the corral before the sun broke over the horizon, navigating the last pathways of shadow on the land before the eye of Man awakened to rule a slow and sultry Saturday in his realm. A forest lay before him.

Oracle found a stand of anacua trees bordering a field with bales of hay. The gulf wind had scattered the ungathered surplus, such that the forest floor beneath the nearest trees was a comfortable bed of straw. Oracle abided under the anacuas, awaiting the visit of the friends with the boy. And the silence of the waiting made space for the colors of the morning to speak the new song of rose, pink, lavender, and gray that breathed in more blue with each breath the sky took.

11

THE VOW

While Oracle rested under anacua trees, Paco rested under mesquite inside a rolling pickup. The F-250 rocked along the two ruts marking the way home. A whip-poor-will flew up from a hedge of whitebrush on the roadside, veered off, and disappeared. Paco's breath fogged the spot on the window where he watched the passing forest.

Tío José leaned upon the steering wheel. "We'll be getting back right on time today. We've caught enough tilapia for Tía to work her noonday magic. What a good fisherman you are, son! As good as that great blue heron who kept an eye on us the whole time we were out there. You have learned how to cast, and it shows!"

Paco turned and smiled. "Casting was so fun! When my papá fished with me near Mérida, he covered my hands with his own and we cast together, but today I learned to cast all by myself!"

"You have grown and learned. Your papá would be proud of you, mijo."

"Each time the line pulled with a fish it made me scared and happy at the same time!"

Tío José smiled wistfully. "A happy kind of scared: That's a good way to put it. A *miedo alegre,* a joyful fear that gave you strength to bring each fish in! You didn't lose a single one after you learned how to set the hook!"

Paco made a champion's gesture with his arms and high-fived Tío José.

The vaquero motioned with his head to the truck bed. "And fish aren't all we are bringing home for Tía. With those chili peppers we picked up from Raphael on the way here, she will have all she needs for her mole poblano. There's no sauce like it in all the Valley, mijo. It takes her two days to make, son, *two whole days*! But once you taste it, you'll feel like you've eaten the fruit of Eden! She won't let me in the kitchen when she's making it. She says I eat too much of it, but I tell her I'm *not* eating it; I'm only *tasting* it! So, I've seen from the doorway the bounty that goes into it. Chocolate and chilis! Cinnamon and sesame! Tomatoes and tomatillos!"

Paco smacked his lips. "Wow, I'm hungry!"

"Oh, but that's not all: There's grapes and garlic! Cumin and cloves! Pine nuts and pecans and a dash of *hoja santa*—oh, it will keep you eating! Just look at how well-fed *I* am. That sauce will turn your meal into muscle!"

And the vaquero slapped his belly as Paco laughed.

Tío José turned west onto a caliche road reaching to the horizon through the mesquite. The road and the strip of land on either side connected Eden's Bend to the eastern coastal mangrove marshes. The vaquero glanced at the signs of the fishing expedition smudged upon the boy.

"Take the towel and wipe down your feet, son," he said with a mock frown. "And take those water shoes off so you dry out your feet. Tía won't let you in the trailer before we clean up. The wading was worth it to get to the fishing hole; the good catch will make Tía happy. I'm the only one who knows about that freshwater spring coming up on the far side of the mangroves beyond the road. That's where the fish hide, and that's where they bite! Now you know the secret too! But

Tía won't care how many secrets we tell her if we don't wash off first. We won't eat without clean feet."

With the big toe of each foot, Paco removed the water shoes, which were still damp from wading. He took the towel, warmed by the sun inside the truck, and removed the pieces of mangrove debris the water had left stuck to his skin. He cleaned the silt from between his toes and slumped back with a sigh of contentment. Tree after tree passed by the window as the truck carried him deeper into Eden's Bend.

Paco felt around in his pocket. He fished out a marble and lifted it before his eyes.

Tío José noticed. "Ah, is that the one you chose to take with you today?"

"Yes, I chose this one for today."

"Why that one?"

"It was the one I saved in the water that night."

Tío José's face registered the phrase. "Oh...oh, yes. That night...I'm sorry, son. I didn't think about that when I took you out there to the estuary. It was your first time in the water since—that night, yes?"

"No, it wasn't."

"It wasn't? When have you gone wading in the water?"

"I didn't wade. I swam. I was with my friends. We swam under a little bridge. We followed the water trail of the resacas."

"Who were your friends who swam with you?"

"The raccoon and the good cat."

Tío José looked at the boy, glancing up at the road just enough to keep the truck on it.

"You swam...with 'the raccoon and the good cat'...I see... hmm...the raccoon you came with?"

"Yes, he likes to swim. So does the good cat. We swam together."

"A…raccoon and a cat swam together with you? I know raccoons like to dip their paws in the water—it's as if they are washing their food! And I know they can swim. But to swim with a cat? And to swim with you? That's new."

Tío José lifted a hand off the wheel in an open gesture. "And as for a *cat* who likes to swim, I have never seen it myself. House cats don't normally do that. Of course, the ocelot and the bobcat are good swimmers: *el ocelote* and *el gato montés*—and the otter cat, too, but no one has seen one of those for a lifetime in the Valley. My papá called the otter cat *el gato colorado*. He called it the jaguarundi too. That cat was invisible, a friend to farmers through the mice it caught. But the jaguarundi never heard a 'gracias' for his service, for he never showed himself to them."

Paco cradled the marble. "I do not know about the otter cat, but I do know about the good cat. We were friends. He asked me to tell him my story, so I did. He helped me get well. So did the raccoon and the bird that let me touch his head. But the bird did not swim. He flew. He made me tea with the help of the raccoon."

Tío José stopped looking at the road and let the truck coast. He searched the boy's eyes.

Is he joking? Hallucinating? Or perhaps it's trauma…No, I see no injury in his eyes, no fear or phantom at play. Only…purity…

Tío José returned to driving, but slower. "I…see. You are brave then, Little Colt. Braver than me. And deeper. Before now I had not asked you about the water. If I had, you would have told me your story. You would have told me about your friend the…good cat. And the other good ones too, like the bird who let you touch his head. And your friend the raccoon, of course. I would have learned about them swimming with you. I would have learned that the memory of the water is a long story only you know, both the bad and the good. Forgive me, son. Forgive me."

"How did you know my name?"

"What?"

"How did you know my name?"

"What do you mean? Your name is Paco."

"You said 'Little Colt.' That's what Mamá and Papá called me."

Tío José frowned thoughtfully. "Ah, yes, I did say that, didn't I? Well, I don't really know. I don't know why I said that. It just came to mind. I just came upon it like that freshwater spring beneath the mangroves. Before I knew it, I was there."

In the quiet that followed, the rhythm of the truck's diesel engine played a slow antiphony with the passing trees, becoming stronger in sound before the thicker ones and gentler before the thinner ones as the truck passed them.

"I forgive you, Tío…I forgive you."

"Thank you…son."

"When Mamá and Papá called me *Potrillo*, it was always with a smile. How can I not forgive you when you know my name? And besides, I had everything I needed in the water of the fishing hole. You were with me—you who know my name—and the marble was with me, the marble from the sea. It was enough."

Tío José touched Paco's shoulder. "Sorry we could not bring all the marbles—Little Colt. I didn't want them accidentally spilling while we were out there in the marshes. Better to cherish one and miss the rest than to cherish all and lose them all. It's better for the heart."

Paco contemplated the marble he had chosen. The silent planet held within it another world, sacred and preserved inside the glassy gray-green stone, a hidden treasure revealed but not explained.

Tío José turned an AC vent toward the child. "You love your marbles, don't you? It is good you made a level playing field for them outside. I know you've tried and tried to play with them on the trailer floor, but when the wind blows, our trailer moves, and the marbles move too. They don't sit still but sooner or later rush away like a frightened crowd to one end of the room or the other. Such is how the wind plays with an old metal home on wheels and jack posts. But no amount of shaking can keep you from picking up one treasure at a time, son, and you do that well. Yes, Little Colt, you do that quite well, and no one will take that away from you. No one."

"Not even Tío Sergio?" Paco asked as he hid the marble in his pocket. "He told you, 'Don't become too attached to the child.'"

A shock flashed across Tío José's face, though he managed to keep looking forward. "How did you know that?"

"I listened."

"What?"

"I listened to you and Tía. After we came home with my new shoes yesterday, you sat with her and drank limonada by the fan. You always sit there after doing something. You sit there and you talk."

Tío swung his head. "I thought you were playing marbles behind the sunflowers!"

"I was. But I don't need my ears for that. They can do something else while my eyes are busy."

Tío gave a look of embarrassment. "Oh, of course. Just because you are turned away from us doesn't mean you can't hear us. 'Little jars have big ears,' as they say. It is true, Potrillo. You are the child we are attached to. You are the one El Dragón wants. He is angry. Angry and hungry."

Paco felt the marble in his pocket. He looked at the bird-less sky. "I do not like El Dragón."

Tío drove in silence for a time. "Neither do I, Little Colt. Neither do I."

"Will he take me?"

"He will try, but not now, mijo. Not now. Remember, El Dragón is named after a reptile. And what is a reptile, my son? It is a cold-blooded thing."

"The blood in El Dragón is cold? Like the ice chest for the tilapia?"

"Not exactly, son. The blood in El Dragón is 'cold' because he depends on favorable conditions before he makes his move. When it is not favorable, he lies still and waits."

"Is there favor now?"

"No, mijo, no…there is not. You are safe anywhere on Eden's Bend. That Tío Sergio is El Dragón's eyes and ears, but he cannot be his hands and feet. Those are bound…for now. There is no favor for El Dragón on this ranch, any more than a snake has favor during a winter frost."

Paco touched Tío's elbow. "But what happens when the frost ends? What happens when the cold blood in El Dragón can move him?"

Tío faced straight ahead, slowing the truck to a stop. As he looked out, he grew sober and still. He took a deep breath and turned to Paco, who noticed that Tío's eyes were wet with tears, though his forehead bore sweat as if he had just forged a sword on an anvil.

He placed an arm around Paco. "Little Colt, don't you worry 'bout a thing. You will not be alone on that day. You will never be alone again, hear me? I will be with you and your tía will be with you. If El Dragón comes for you, we will stand in his way. He will have to deal with us first."

Tío leaned forward. His face glowed as if the light of an unseen torch touched him from an uplifted arm before a fanged foe in the dead of night. He whispered, but his voice was strong and unwavering.

"I will defend you, son. Yes, I will defend you from El Dragón."

He placed his hands over those of the boy.

"I swear it."

While Paco and Tío traveled home in conversation, Patch traveled the trail of the jaguar across Eden's Bend. He followed the scent and enjoyed unusual safety in the daylight, for it was the Saturday before the Fourth of July, and all but a skeleton crew of ranch hands were gone. Manmachines were at rest and gave the raccoon hiding places where he could plan his next move across open ground. At midday, Patch crossed the field of hay bales and found Oracle lying among the anacua trees where they met the leftover straw strewn on the ground like a light carpet.

The lord of the Valley welcomed Patch with a smile as the raccoon reclined beside him.

Oracle rested his paw upon a tuft of hay. "I am told I will eat clover one day, and I suppose, therefore, this straw."

Patch sniffed the straw and nibbled a piece of it. "Hmm. Not much flavor. Who told you that, sire?"

"A cunning giver of riddles who held the clue to where the jaguarundi will be. I met her just before the dread battle with my cougar-cousin who gave me this scar on the land of a kind hermit named Brazos Ben."

"Who was she, a coyote? A raven? Those tribes can be pretty tricky."

"No, she was a coral snake who lived in the manplace of a fisherman's ghost."

"A fisherman's ghost! Yikes! You had quite an adventure in your travels up north. Ghosts and snakes and cougars: I sure wouldn't want to meet any of those! And you met all three!"

"Yes, I did. And though I had no desire to meet any of them, I needed to meet all of them, or I would not be here. But of all my encounters, the one with the coral was key for recovering a lost treasure to the Valley, for she carried the clue for finding the shadow cat."

Patch absentmindedly set pieces of straw side by side. "I can't say I've had much luck in conversations with corals. Charming colors I must say: deep crimson and sunshine yellow and a shiny black as deep as the coat button in my treasure pouch! Almost as attractive as marbles, and there's no coat of colors like 'em—Oh, except for the king snake, of course. Forgot about them. They look like coral snakes at first glance. I don't think the king snake is a close relative of the coral, but his colors are just like hers, except in a different order. My tribe chants a song at the Rite of the Fourth Ring so we'll remember how to tell the difference. Comes in handy if we find ourselves with one and aren't sure which set of teeth we're dealing with.

> *Red and yellow kill a fellow*
> *Red and black's a friendly jack*
> *The order of the stripes will show*
> *Whether you greet friend or foe*

Then you'll live a little longer
Outmaneuver poison stronger
Never linger with a coral
Nor forget our story's moral

Oracle laughed. "I am confident there is not a single member of the House of Procyon in the Valley who has ever mistook a friend from foe among kings and corals. To put a word to song is to store it in the deepest place of the heart, for there, in the deepest place, is the home of poems and rhymes and songs."

Patch put the row of straw stems under his paw. "Why do you think that is, sire?"

Oracle looked up at the sky through the anacua leaves. "I cannot say for sure, Fair Bandit, but I wonder if it is because the heart of the Maker sings too. Perhaps when He made all things, He sang them into being."

Patch cocked his head. "Huh. Wow, sire, you sure think things through more than I do. But I reckon you're on to something, 'cause whenever I or any of my kind go about our business and feel it's fine to let our guard down, we hum tunes, sometimes a song from the Rites of the Rings, sometimes just something we make up without so much as a single conscious thought. It just sort of happens, like a birds on one end of the woods picking up the song of a bird on the other end."

Oracle leaned his head toward Patch. "Sort of like one calling to another."

Patch nodded, his face reflective. "Yeah, I guess you could say that. It's like…well, it's like the Maker never stopped singing."

Oracle smiled. "Fascinating, Fair Bandit. Now, I think *you* are on to something."

And after a lovely nap for both cat and coon while the wind whispered songs through the leaves of the trees, Patch bid the lord of the Valley farewell to summon Miracle with the friends.

12

THE ENCOUNTER

Little Colt and Tío José reached the tree-lined entrance to the trailer park, where retamas—that same palo verde of Patch's surname—welcomed them. A pair of summer tanagers flitted from the top of one as they passed, the male a rosy red, the female in plumage of mustard yellow and olive green. A red-shouldered hawk surprised them, waiting to launch from its branch next to the road until, when it did, it swooped low across the hood. The vaquero hit the brakes and both he and the boy lurched forward, grabbing the dashboard. The two laughed with joy at the startle.

They parked beneath the canopy of their turquoise trailer, a square of shade in the heat of the day. Tía Lourdes took her stand at the screen door when they stepped out of the truck.

"Go wash that marsh water off of you! No one enters here until he's hosed himself down!"

Tío José doffed his hat and bowed with a flourish.

"But, dulce dama, we have already wiped down with a towel."

"You mean that same towel that's been rotting in your truck since the chili cook-off on Cinco de Mayo? You probably *put* dirt on yourselves instead of wiping it off. Now get over there and hose down. You men clean up till there's not a speck of mud or mangrove on you. I just mopped the floor, and I don't want my work wasted. While you clean yourselves and clean the fish, I will get ready the lemon butter, the peppercorn, and everything else."

"Sí, señora," the vaquero said with a bow of the head. He lowered the tailgate and placed the cooler full of fish on it, along with the knife for cleaning them.

At the place where the shadow of the awning met the sunshine, Paco poured water down his legs with a green garden hose. Tío José peeled off his sweaty socks, standing barefoot on a patch of grass while he scraped mud off his neoprene waders with an old mason's spatula.

"Son, if we pass the interviews, Marshal Freeman says we might be together a long time, long enough for me to see you grow up and long enough for you to see me forget my name! Ha! Who would have thought that a couple with no children would have to learn how to raise one when their hair is gray!"

The thoughts released by the wonder of Tío José filled the silence. The sound of running water soaked those thoughts and held them there like a cloud awaiting the wind. Paco leaned his lips into the glistening arch of water, a cool stream flavored with the hose.

"This tastes like Mérida," he whispered.

At that moment, a neotropic cormorant flew at the level of Tío José's head. He turned, but the bird had pulled up to circle above the canopy, where his swift shadow disappeared.

Tía Lourdes called from the trailer screen door, her staff sergeant scowl replaced with a grandmotherly grin. "Now, then, since you are finally taking care of yourselves properly, I can officially say, '¡Bienvenidos, fishermen!'"

A scratching sound on the truck roof turned all heads; the cormorant was there. He clucked a series of staccato sounds.

Tía Lourdes put a hand on her hip. "Does he hope for a fish from the cooler?"

The cormorant hopped down and landed before Paco, staring into the boy's face with his aquamarine eye and giving his call again, a sort of homely croak like the last drops passing through a steaming coffee maker. Then he skimmed the ground a brief distance in the direction of the corral where Paco's friends lived. He landed beside a tussock of wild rye, turned to Paco, and called again. He opened his wings and remained perfectly still.

Paco shut off the hose and put it down. "I do not think he wants fish just now, Tía. I think he wants me to follow him."

Tío José pulled on his socks, hopping a couple of wobbly steps as he did so. "You cannot go alone."

"I am not alone. The bird is with me."

"I mean you cannot go without *me*."

Tía Lourdes stepped out of the trailer. She squinted, analyzing of the bird, who once again called the clumsy clarion of his kind. Then, out of the wild rye, appeared the raccoon.

Tía Lourdes laid a hand on the side of her face as if giving it a gentle slap. "Your friend too? Mystery! Strange things surround our son. Too amazing to be afraid of, too good to be true. What do we do?"

Paco stepped toward the meadow. "I know what to do! I must go to them. They are waiting for me."

Tío José pulled the loop on a work boot to sink his heel in. "*Mi querida,* let's save the fish until tonight's meal. I will go with Paco now. We will be home by supper—right, Potrillo? Home by supper? We don't want your Tía's hard work and clean house to go wasted."

Tía Lourdes did a double take toward her husband. "What did you just call him? 'Potrillo'?"

"Oh…yes, I did!" He tipped his hat. "Señora Benavides, meet El Potrillo."

The child laughed. "I'll be home by supper, Tía. I promise."

"All right…Potrillo."

Tío José and Paco went to Patch and the cormorant. The boy placed his hand on the raccoon, who bowed at the boy's touch. The cormorant hopped onto the boy's shoulder, balancing his perch with wings and tail. The bird looked about in the same way he searched the shallows for minnows. Then, having turned toward the direction where the corral lay, he sprang into the shimmering summer air.

Tío José shook his head as he marveled. "I know you spend time with your friends at the corral, but to have a bird calling you to go there, that is new to me."

Little Colt laughed again. "They always show me something new. Like the marbles when I play."

Having crossed the pastureland with the raccoon to reach the corral, vaquero and son found the cormorant sitting on a fence post. Beside him was the horse, head dipping over the fence toward the boy, nodding him a welcome.

"They seem eager to tell you something," said Tío José.

"They always are," the child replied, "but it takes time to listen. I give them time."

The horse recognized Tío José as the Man who had tended his hooves on the day they met and, from that day on, had allowed him to rest in the shade while the manchild Miracle played. He received the Man's touch to his forehead.

The vaquero smiled as he stroked the horse's neck. "How are you, weary traveler? Good to see you. I am glad you are getting the rest and feed you need."

The raccoon grasped the horse's tail and climbed to his back. He looked at the Man and the boy.

Tío José smiled. "Just like the day we met."

The horse turned toward the gate, nuzzling it. Paco saw and, with the help of that gate as a stepping stool, climbed upon the back of the beast of burden. The cormorant flew away with a whoosh of wings just over everyone's heads, and as he did, a Gulf Coast toad called from the horse's mane. The child turned to his guardian.

"Tío, I have to go with them."

"Where to?"

"They will show me."

"I will go with you."

Tío José saddled a palomino who, along with several other horses, were Plod's neighbors in the stable that had replaced his original home. When the vaquero emerged, he found Plod waiting for him outside the corral with his three passengers.

"How did you do that, Potrillo?"

"Do what?"

"Open the corral gate?"

"The horse knows how."

"Oh...he knows how...I see. You didn't get down and open the gate?"

"No, Tío, it was just like I said. The horse opened it."

"Well, he's quite a smart horse if he can do that. He must remember things about his kind I have never learned! But come now, let us go wherever you think your friends need to take you so we can return to Tía soon."

—⟋⟋⟋—

In the air around Oracle, the anacua trees murmured as a breeze passed through them. The leaves, sandpaper-rough, gave a sound like surf on the shore as they slid back and forth upon each other, speaking the stories the roots retained. Oracle took in the stories. He watched a family of tortoise beetles tending their work on the tree closest to him, where they harvested the last of the year's berries in colors red and yellow-orange. Oracle could smell their late-bloom aromas. He took in the smell and the ripe promise it carried.

Presently, the reclining jaguar felt a slight vibration in the earth beneath him.

Horses approach.

Their sound reached him beyond the tree line, then stopped. The summer breeze shifted, carrying to him the scent of horses, a toad, a raccoon, and Man. Oracle rose.

"The anacua trees pour out a yes in their whispers," he said softly.

"We do," an anacua replied, "for it has been many springs since a lord of the Valley reclined here, and many more springs since a gathering like this took place. There is peace for all to be present."

"This is the arrival of the manchild whom I have befriended. Both he and I are far from our homes in the Southern Jungle. Both he and I have found family here, though at a cost, and the child has paid the greater. But I am at home with him, and he with me, and this is a lifelong consolation."

The anacua whispered through a rustling of leaves. "If the child is at home with you, then he is of a rare mantribe, a kind of friend and a kind of family seldom seen under the sun."

"Yes," Oracle replied, "he is a forerunner of the fellowship to come. A first bloom of a final spring before the everlasting one."

Tío José followed the friends. Miracle led them across the meadow of mown grass and hay bales to the tree line of the wilderness, where branches of anacua veiled the unseen realm beyond them.

"We shall go in here, Tío," said Paco.

"There are wild things in there, son."

"I know, but I have my friends."

Tío José frowned. He took off his hat and ran his weathered fingers through his hair. He looked to the right and to the left as if seeking advice. Then he looked at the four-footed ones with the boy.

"Well, they brought you through it before; I guess they could bring you through it again. But it is different this time. I am here. I cannot leave you."

The sound of a truck caused all to turn. Tía Lourdes arrived, a soft plume of dust rising behind the F-250. She stepped out of the truck fumbling with a hair clip, which she worked with until she had tamed the wisps of her semi-colored hair. She took a deep breath, smoothed down her clothes, and beheld the gathering of loved ones and animals.

She went and stood beside her husband's palomino. "I had to come. Our supper can wait."

Tío José turned to the child. "We will stay here awhile, Potrillo. Then we will either go home or come retrieve you. I do not know. It seems too wrong to leave you but too beyond us to follow you. We will wait here until we know what to do."

Without a word and without breaking her gaze on the friends, the hand of Tía Lourdes found that of her husband, who had let one hand off the reins and dropped it to his side.

Tía Lourdes sighed. "All right, I'm ready to wait and see too."

Suddenly, an aplomado falcon landed on Tío José's shoulder. He startled and instinctively threw up his hands to shoo the bird away. Tía Lourdes gave a brief shout of surprise. The falcon held on, spreading out his wings and giving the call of his kind. The vaquero's hat fell off.

He swung a hand onto the rim of the saddle to steady himself. "What is this? Another friend? He has sharp fingers!"

Paco's laughter was like a song. "He is the one who let me touch his head! He helped make the tea I drank that made me feel better. He is part of the family of birds who go with us."

Tío José stared warily at the bird of prey, unable to move his head farther back from the falcon than his neck would allow. But the falcon, for his part, looked only at the child, paying no attention to the anxious face beside him.

"Oh, I see," said Tío slowly. "This family of birds who go with us; they are like your angels, yes?"

"I guess so," Paco said. "I guess they are my angels."

"The *cormorán* too? The one who landed on the truck?"

"The cormorán too."

"He's a fisherman with an angel's job!"

"I am not sure he ever forgets about fish while he is being an angel too. He is a friend who likes to fish, just like the good cat."

"The good cat likes to fish, eh?"

"Yes, and he is really good."

"So, I guess he doesn't eat you if he is full of fish."

"No, he does not."

"He does not, hmm. Maybe the birds help him find the fish."

"I do not see them looking for fish for the good cat, but I do see them looking for me."

"Ah, ¡claro! The birds take turns at their work of protecting you. I pray to Saint Michael every day for his protection, but he always does his work without me seeing him. *You*, on the other hand, get to *see* your angels. You are a blessed boy."

Paco smiled. "I need to go now if I am to keep my promise to Tía."

The vaquero exhaled with a look of reluctant resignation. "Yes…yes, I guess you do. Now that I have seen you have a family of angels keeping watch over you, I think we can go back to the trailer with a clear conscience. I will be on the patio waiting for you, son."

"¡Gracias, Tío y Tía!"

The branches of the anacua stirred at a place where the berries hung in clusters as thick as a beaded curtain. Oracle appeared.

Tía Lourdes screamed. *"El tigre!* God help us!" She stumbled toward the truck while Tío struggled with his panicked horse.

But Miracle leaped off Plod and ran to Oracle, throwing himself upon him. Together they tumbled, a tangle of arms, legs, and fur. The jaguar hopped up, gamboled a circle around the boy, and hunkered into a playful pose, legs poised like tightened springs while his tail lashed his body, as if daring the child to chase him. The boy laughed, Oracle roared, Plod neighed, Patch squealed, and Bog croaked. Again, and again, each beast sounded the call of its kind, a cacophony becoming harmony by the high voice of the happy child that bound the sounds together.

Tío José's palomino reared as he reined it in. "¡Ay, Dios mío! Lourdes! Get the rifle from the truck! Now!"

"No, Tío, no!" laughed Paco. "This is my friend, the good cat! My friend, the good cat!"

And the boy the birds named Miracle jumped out of the jumble only to have Patch leap upon his chest. Gladly did the boy fall backward upon the weary grass, tumbling and giggling while the raccoon tickled the manchild's face with his whiskers. Up the boy jumped again, throwing his arms around the neck of the horse. And, from within Plod's sweaty mane, Bog intoned a heraldic proclamation to capture the memory of the moment.

Tío and Tía beheld the joy beyond the reach of the world of reins and rifles. Miracle and his friends turned to face them, their eyes calm, their bodies steady, their breathing slightly heavy from the frolic. The boy beamed.

Still gripped in fright at the sight of the jaguar, the palomino stumbled backward with every muscle tensed to flee, ears flat, nostrils flared. He whinnied high and raised his head as Tío José fought to restrain him.

Plod turned to the palomino and lifted up his voice in the authority of one who knows his friends. The old horse whinnied the words of secret speech known only to the House of Equus. The palomino paused, put at ease by the testimony of his older brother about the Cat Who Remembers. He backed up again slightly (for his momentum still moved him in that direction) then stilled himself. The look of panic gave way to curiosity as the palomino threw his ears forward.

Tío José looked on with wonder. "¿Qué es esto?"

Paco laughed as if a piñata had just broken open above his head. "The good cat has come back! My friend, the good cat! The cat the raccoon led me to. The cat who sat with me while I drank the tea. The cat who said to me, 'Tell me your story.' The moon will laugh when she sees us together! She will laugh and not lose heart! For though Mamá and Papá have gone far away, look who has come back, but you, good cat, my friend, and all my friends who helped me escape the dark shadows!"

Tía Lourdes whispered prayers.

Tío José said prayers, too, but without words, his prayers spoken through eyes brimming with tears. "Little Colt, I—I— son, it's a miracle!"

"'Dark shadows'…?" Tía Lourdes asked with a quavering voice. "*They* are why you are alive?"

"Yes, Tía, they brought me food when I fainted. They saved me from the dogs in the night. They freed me from the rancher who caught me with a rope. Papá Eli helped me, too, when he brought me to you. And now I have found you *and* I have found my friends I had lost. *¡Yupi!*"

"How did you tame them?" Tía Lourdes asked.

"Tame them? I do not know what you mean."

Tío José cleared his throat. "She means, how did you keep them from biting you?"

"I did not tame them, but they did not bite me either. I do not know why. All I know is that I found them, and they found me."

The Man and the Woman took it in, Little Colt standing among his friends while they abided in leisurely repose around Miracle. The boy communed with them in a fellowship silent and full. It was the full silence of the early morning, as when dew gathers on grass before the rays of dawn discover it. It was the full silence of a cloud of incense, a cloud you can smell but not grasp, for the cloud surrounds you. It was the full silence of discovery, as when a climber reaches the snowbound peak and sees three countries from the solid footing of a single, majestic stone. Such was the communion between the boy and the friends, and such was the communion of the old souls who beheld them.

The boy understood his place. His face shone with irrefutable joy.

"I must go with them, Tía. I have to. They are on their way somewhere, looking for something. I do not know what they are looking for, but if I am with them, I will know. They helped me on my journey. I must help them on theirs."

Tío José pushed his chin into the space between his thumb and forefinger, the hand pushing his cheeks upward to support his undone stare. "I have only heard of these things in stories. I have never seen them with my eyes. This is a mystery I cannot solve."

"I am not sure we are supposed to solve it," said his wife with tears on her cheeks. "I think we are just supposed to receive it."

The vaquero let out a sharp breath. "But, son, you cannot go! You are alone!"

Paco laughed. "How can I be alone when my friends are with me? I will never be alone."

"But, son—I mean you are going without us. It is not right!"

Paco scratched Oracle behind his ear. The jaguar stretched his neck toward the boy in the comfort he gave him, eyes closed in delight as any cat would do. The sight was so placid, so quiet yet full, that Tío José felt himself a stranger in another world.

"I am new to these things I see. I cannot deny what is before me, but how can I trust such a thing to be?"

"Only by letting us go, Tío. I will come back once I have helped my friends find what they are looking for, and when I do, you will know you did the right thing."

The animals reclined, Plod pulling on a tuft of grass, Patch cleaning his paws with his tongue, Oracle flopping on his side in complete ease as if he were a house cat on the back porch on a summer day. Slowly, the scene soaked into the old couple like rainwater on clothing, which, with gentle persistence, eventually penetrates even the most waterproof of overcoats. And the Man and the Woman continued to absorb the gathering, as much as they could bear, until it seemed to them their hearts were breaking—not in desolation, but as when the hull of a seed splits open to reveal the life growing there.

Tía lifted her glistening eyes, whispering. "Yes, you should go, but you will promise to return by the time the sun sets. Dinner will be waiting."

"I promise, Tía! I will come back when the sun sets! Then we will feast. You will see!"

The falcon cried the call of his kind and launched from Tío José's shoulder, sailing through the branches with such finesse that it was as if the branches were not there at all. The friends followed. Tío and Tía watched in silent, still anticipation, as when worshippers wait for the priest to return from the inner sanctum, knowing that the bread he brings them from that hidden place will be blessed with life-giving grace.

13

THE TURTLES SPEAK

Sent flew ahead of the friends. He landed in a leafless oak rising above the rest of the trees, a dormant watch tower stretching out its barren branches. The falcon cried a *klee-klee-klee* as the friends reached the foot of the tree.

Oracle called up to him. "Hail, Airborne Counselor. What does your sharp sight see? Are there turtles?"

"Yes, sire," the aplomado replied. "The drought has drawn them together to the resacas that remain. Having said farewell to many a pond and creek now sleeping before the barren sky, they gather in groups among the remaining waterways, groups three and four generations deep."

"I must speak with them."

"The turtles will not welcome your coming, sire. One look at you and, in the blink of an eye, they will disappear into the heart of the pond."

Oracle wound and unwound his tail around his body. "You are quite right. It is a riddle we must solve before we see them."

The friends continued deeper into the forest, passing no words, savoring the presence of one another. They made their way through the trees wherever the palmettos grew thinnest and the prairie sumac had dried.

After a time, they came to a clearing where a shallow pond lay breathing its last. Many a footprint led to the water's edge and away again. Among the spoor were the unmistakable tracks of the turtles. The foot marks were ovals, and each featured five terrapin claw marks. Through some tracks a gently curving line bore witness to the tail. Other tracks showed where the shells dragged the soil in a regular rhythm. One set of tracks was much larger than the others.

Oracle paused beside them, letting out a slow, soft growl.

Miracle rested his hand on him. "What is it, good cat?"

The jaguar placed his muzzle upon the turtle tracks and followed them two paces. Turning, he looked at the boy and waited.

Miracle considered the tracks. "Do these speak to you? Do they show you the way you need to go to find the thing you are looking for?" The boy bent down and traced the mark of a turtle's tail with his fingers. "They are thirsty. The water here is almost gone. I bet they have gone to see their cousins where the ponds are deeper. I will pick up the trail for you. Follow me."

The child led, and the friends followed. They passed between yaupon growing in the shade of tall trees. Then they came to a thicket where branches hung so low that Miracle and Plod could not walk directly alongside the turtle trail. The good cat took the lead again until they were in the clear, and he and the raccoon waited while the horse and his boy went around. Bog remained in Plod's mane, watchful and in thought, storing up the memory of the day for a volume of poems to come.

Katydids and grasshoppers leaped away with an annoyed whirr of their wings as the friends progressed. Cicadas raised a chorus as the heat of the day reached its peak.

"This forest has lost the grace of hospitality for travelers," Bog said. "Oh for the Pink Moon of spring to come again! Maybe then there will be rain."

A mockingbird guarding a bush of wild Turk's cap squawked at them and flew off.

"Yep," Plod said. "Kindness has tuckered out for bush and bird alike. That mockingbird doesn't know our food is this journey. We won't eat his store. We could have invited him to come with us if he had lingered a little longer. Then he would have had quite a tale to tell creation. He could have helped the falcon too. Mockingbirds love to gossip, but there's always a nugget or two of useful knowledge if you're patient enough to put up with the fluff."

Miracle tracked the turtle trail as it wound in a slow serpentine pattern. The friends, likewise, followed the S-curve the turtle tribes had left behind. They reached a place where the foliage before them was so thick and green that nothing could be seen beyond it.

A slight breeze began to blow, bringing with it the scent of water. Oracle stopped and gave a thoughtful growl. Miracle heard and turned to him. The jaguar sat down, forelegs straight like gentle poles, hind legs forming a base around which his tail curled. The horse and the toad halted beside him while the raccoon came to the boy and did the same.

Miracle knelt to eye level with Oracle. "What is it, good cat?"

The tip of the jaguar's tail danced playfully. Then he opened his mouth, and, though the child heard no words with his ears, his heart comprehended them:

How do you welcome sight unseen?
How may the turtles linger?
How may the hardened shell turn soft?
It must behold the singer

And with that, Oracle sang. A fresh, flowing tone began to make its way through the trees toward the yet-unseen pond.

The dark enclosed a sojourner
The drought a pilgrim passing
The day disclosed a neighbor new
With friendship for the asking

The spotted wanderer has come
With eyes set on the finding
Of guides to where the secrets live
Beyond the path he's winding

On the other side of the trees, on the limbs of a fallen, barkless ash marooned in a resaca, the turtles listened. They were from six tribes, pressed together into branch-shaped rows by the drought that had gradually corralled them.

The heart of the ash took in the moment, holding it in the essence of her wood, such that long after the drought had broken and the resaca had returned to its prime as a perch-rich oasis, the memory of that moment sang to minnow and tadpole alike from the exuding oils of the sunken tree:

A slider, a cooter, a Cagle's map traveler
A softshell, a tortoise with yellow-gray dome
We listened, we pondered the unseen sojourner
Each one in the heart of his terrapin home

The singer he touched us inside our encasements
Where cardiac chambers had hidden a song
A chorus forgotten like boxes in basements
Discovered by relatives after you're gone

A musing and rising of old memoranda
Like spiraling out of dank turreted stairs
That break into daylight and full panorama
An instant ago you were quite unawares

The singer assailed not our hardened position
Protecting ourselves with a shield and a hole
Instead he has conquered our hearts with a vision
That already rested inside of our souls

The turtles lifted their heads, and as they did, they became more still than when they were basking. For in the stillness of basking only, the heart wanders between dreams, desires, cares, and slumber. But the stillness of listening commands the heart to wander no more. And in the same way that water reflects a more perfect picture of the sky when the ripples cease, even so, the listening heart sees more clearly when holding back the four winds that would otherwise blow upon it. Such was the stillness the turtles entered into as they listened to the song.

After giving the music a moment to linger after he had sung it, Oracle rose, approached the manchild, and bowed before him.

Miracle placed his hands on Oracle's shoulders. "Good cat, I see you must do something. I bless you to do it. Yes, I do." And the child kissed the cat on his forehead.

Oracle bowed again, approached the veil of foliage, and entered. On the other side, he appeared at the bank of the resaca.

—w—

The turtles beheld the cat of the Southern Jungle, but they did not dive into the water. A young one, a red-eared slider, spoke first, for it is customary in the House of Cheloniidae that the turtle who has seen more suns than the rest remains silent until all others have had their say, and thus the oldest one has the final word.

"You who show no teeth to us," cried the young slider, "tell us why you sing."

"Yes, tell us," said a Cagle's map turtle, his shell vivid with dark-olive lines like the contours of mountains on a map. "For we saw you with our ears before we saw you with our eyes, and we decided to remain until our eyes could agree with our ears. Yours is not the song of a hunter."

A Rio Grande river cooter raised her head. "You have hunger of a different kind, one that does not devour turtles."

"Your insight is true, Ponderers of the Ponds," Oracle replied. "I am not here to devour, but to discover. I will show you what I seek."

Oracle lifted his right paw to show the skin pads of its underside, each one framed with fur. His claws were velveted. Then he stretched forth his paw, and in the soft earth where the resaca bank met the water, he drew the sign the coral snake had shown him in the manrealm of Brazos Ben: the manletter *B* within in a square set at the angle of a diamond.

The turtles stretched their necks as the symbol took form before them; they stretched even more to take it in once Oracle had finished. Their eyes grew wide. For a moment they were motionless. Only the discerning eye would have seen that the motionlessness was not the freezing of timidity but the solemn pause preceding the moment of a great decree.

It was an alligator snapping turtle who, eventually, took up the task of giving words to their silent ruminations. For he was the Old One, greater in years and larger than the rest, some two hundred fifty pounds of shell and flesh in a form reminiscent of prehistoric times when his ancestors had seen the rise and fall of monstrous beasts while his tribe remained. He slid off the fallen trunk into the water and swam toward the cat. His shell was covered with rows of spikes, volcanic in shape, his neck with smaller threats equally foreboding. His eyes, small and set behind a sharp beak, remained as fixed on the cat of Sian Ka'an as the periscope of a submarine remains fixed on the ship it is about to send to the bottom of the sea with a dread torpedo.

Patch whispered to Oracle, "Maybe we could talk to him from the tree branches. We're more likely to keep our fur that way. Gosh, sire, he looks like he's as heavy you are!"

Oracle slowly shook his head. "If we retreat to the trees, he will return to the pond. Unless we offer our fur without a fang showing—vulnerable to his bite—he will not speak, for we will not be found worthy of his words."

The snapper came ashore. Miracle backed up a step, Plod beside him doing the same.

"I shall leap upon him!" declared Bog. "Just say the word, sire. It shall be the glorious end I desire."

"No need to leap, Precocious One," Oracle said softly, his eyes remaining on the turtle. "No need for a glorious end today. This is not the time for leaping but for listening."

The snapper looked at no one but the cat. The raccoon remained beside the jaguar but pressed into his side. He could hear Oracle's heartbeat. It was calm.

The ancient reptile stretched out his head from beneath his shell like the bow of a dreadnought leaving its berth. He opened his mouth, the dark talon of his lower jaw gaping away from the other, fixed talon, a fang of a beak before which flesh was as soft as butter before a hot knife. He spoke.

"Hail, Cat of the Southern Jungle. Hail, you who have journeyed far from your tropic home. We see you are not a stranger but a *seeker*. You search for what is forgotten. You look for what is lost. You are thirsty enough to risk a riddle with the coral snake to find it. Thirsty enough to risk returning to dust before the poison serpent and the foe who left his mark in your thigh."

Oracle lifted his head. "I come to pick up the trail where Kahoo the Grave left it. I come to convene a Council of the Cats. And I come to gather the animal kingdom in solemn assembly, that a final season may come when they see honor again and remember their names."

The Old One closed his eyes and swayed his outstretched head. "Kahoo the Grave: that is a name I have not heard for a turtle's age. I knew him. Yes, in my first season on the earth, spikeless and smooth, my eyes fell upon him. Kahoo came to the pond of my parents on a summer night of the falling stars called the Perseids. I watched with wild-eyed wonder as the cat from the House of Panthera Onca drank. Then he kept vigil and considered the stars as they fell. I could not stop looking.

"'Shall I snap him?' I asked in the impudence of youth.

"'No,' Mother replied. 'He is not here to fight. He is here to rule.'

"'And rule he does,' my father said. 'He rules the Valley on both sides of the river, meting out decisions just and fair, and keeping the coyote at bay, that pack-dog who tears into our freshly hatched broods with no warning and no quarter. So be still, my son, and remember this moment. Lay it up in your memory for length of days, for it will serve you well to remember the last jaguar of the Valley: Kahoo the Grave.'"

The Old One opened his eyes and took in every aspect of Oracle's face. "Yes, that is what my father told me, and so it has proved true. His words prepared me for this moment. If you have come to pick up the trail where Kahoo left it, then you have done well, sire, you have done well."

The great snapper moved so close to Oracle that his beak touched his whiskers, and the smell of the pond crept over jaguar and raccoon as the turtle spoke. "But have a care, oh Cat of the Southern Jungle. This is not the realm it used to be. The space between Man and beast is no more. It is crisscrossed by bands of molten earth now hardened—crisscrossed like kudzu vines where both the threat of death and the chance of life tangle together in the arbitrary lordship of Man, so that no one knows from day to day which one will prevail or whether both will color the same sun."

Oracle nodded. "Yes, I know, oh Fearless and Observant One, but those things are beyond my paw. I cannot color the sun with Man's choices any more than I can summon the sun. But I must abide by the trail I have been given under his rays."

"And what is that trail?" the Old One asked.

The Cat Who Remembers turned his head slowly to include Patch, Miracle, Plod, and Bog in a meaningful glance while the beak of the beast brushed the fur at his jugular. Oracle returned his eyes to those of the Old One.

"This is my trail, and the trail of my friends in this hour: to find the jaguarundi. The time has come for him to come out from the shadows where he has long abided with the epithet the coral snakes gave him, the 'shadow cat.' For when he reappears, then the stewards of the Valley will be complete again, the Cats of the Three Tribes. And if the stewards are restored, then a fresh and final spring will come to the Valley, a time when the animals can flourish again in the twilight of the age this side of Eden. A time when the misery of hardship is eclipsed by the mystery of hope."

From deep within the Old One, he murmured a sound somewhere between a hum and a moan. "We know where the shadow cat is, but truly, is the quest worth it to bring him back to the light of day? For Men will hunt you down like they did Kahoo the Grave, and the more you awaken the animal kingdom, the more Man, the Tribe of the Restless Eye, as we call him, will awaken his arbitrary lordship over you, for he will realize that you are on the move. What are the stakes of your quest, that you would risk the long and grasping arm of Man?"

The jaguar touched his forehead to that of the snapper, such that the heart of the resaca on the turtle's breath poured into him, and the breath of Eden's memory began its slow and steady journey to the heart of the terrapin sage.

The lord of the Valley spoke. "Without the jaguarundi, without the shadow cat, the two surviving stewards rule in rivalry with one another, flattening out all matters with arguments and words, forgetting that for each thing that can be known *by* words, there is another thing that is only discovered *without* words. I perceive that the shadow cat will bring that discernment. Then life can flourish again for a time in the Valley. Then dust will live in hope. So, tell me, You Who Fear No Fang, tell me where the jaguarundi is."

The snapper took one lumbering step back, lifted his head, and looked at the whole company of friends.

"A marvel," he said softly. "To think that I would live to see this day and be prepared for it. Oh, bless you, Father and Mother in yon Everlasting Pond, where the shallows are as rich as the depths in that emerald-azure pool, and the reeds are green with the song of spring. Thank you, oh parents, Covering Better than the Hardest Shell. Because of you, I can serve the new lord of the Valley and, through him, the whole of the kingdom:

Rooted and reptilian
Mammal and amphibian
Feathered and four-footed
Humble and hardhearted

Sunshine and torrential rain
Twilight and the path of pain
Full moon and unnumbered stars
Sunrise and redeeming scars

The Old One looked at the lord of the Valley:

"Go northeast to the edge of this manrealm you sojourn, the manrealm Eden's Bend. There, just beyond the border, you will find an abandoned manplace, where Man once poured out rivers of sweat over rivers of fire. But now, in that place, all is as silent as the empty shells of our ancestors."

The turtle looked at the sign on the resaca bank. "You will find this same sign you have drawn in the dirt, but there, it will be standing in the air. It will not have a voice until you take what you see and turn it in your heart. Then it will speak to you. When the sight fills your eyes, you must discern it. And once you have, the sign will speak."

Patch thumped his tail. "This has been mighty helpful, Mr. Snapper! Much obliged. But, what do we do once we've found that sign in the air and turned it in our heart? After it speaks, I mean. What do we do then?"

"Follow the dry creek beds near that sign, oh Procyon's Son. Follow the hollow places of the earth where water once flowed before these days of the sealed sky. If you search far enough, you will find one source still bubbling with life, for a spring persists, seeping through the stones, giving enough water to succor a tree heavily laden with flowers and pods, the tepeguaje, what Man also calls the great leadtree of Mexico. It is there, where the roots meet the stones, that you will find the shadow cat. Stand in the stream and call his name. Though silence be the first reply and empty air the second, wait for the called one to appear. Linger in that stillness, I say, for he will come to you, rest assured. The shadow cat will come."

"Thank you," said Oracle. "As with the allthorn, the cypress, and the willow, under whose branches I have abided; and as with the green jay who chose courage over fear; you too have spoken a map to me as I have abided with you."

The lord of the Valley stood, opened his mouth, and released the memory of Eden upon the turtle tribes gathered on the half-sunken ash. The breath hovered over the pond in an invisible cloud, and, as it lingered, the air became fresh, as if a pocket of springtime had arrived ahead of its fullness. The turtles began to rock their heads in unison. A low note sounded.

"Sire," the raccoon whispered, "is that song coming from the water?"

"No, Patch. Listen closely."

And he did so. "Hmm. Wait! When a turtle pauses to take a breath, there is a change in the sound. Why, it's the turtles—even though not a single mouth of theirs is moving!"

"The deepest songs are the wordless ones, Fair Bandit."

"I think you're right. I guess because they come from the home of words."

"You are on to something again, my friend."

Then, one by one, the turtles slid into the resaca and became an ever-larger circle, swimming counterclockwise, making space for each new swimmer until all were in the aquatic dance. Their humming chorus grew in volume. The ripples of their circle swung out until they bounced from shore, crossed one another, and reverberated upon the turtles' shells, creating a pattern of shapes on the water as complex as lattice windows create in the cool shadows of a Moroccan home. And from the terrapin choir came the memory of what had been in the Days of First Things:

The Namer found us in the night watches
Seeing our tribe's silent observations
Consid'ring our long contemplations
Beholding the turning of moon to dawn
Etching the record thereof in our shells
Keeping the diary of the Maker

The First Man watched us in the morning glow
Taking in our moribund visages
Fixing upon our lumb'ring, somber gait
Discov'ring our noonday rest upon trunks
Fallen across waters like a pier where
We made our gath'ring of shelly domes

"Be wise but unknown," the First Steward said
"Be true but overlooked in the treasure
You carry. Be revealed only to those
Who will go slow, who will go low, who will
Set their will to seek until they find your
Instruction timed only for those who wait."

14

MIRACLE GIVES THE IRON A VOICE

The turtles thanked the jaguar, who bowed in reply. "I am indebted to you," Oracle said, "as is the whole Valley. And the Valley is indebted to a servant from a far country it shall never know, a wounded warrior removed from glory who yet did a good thing for the glory of others. Crash the tiger is his name. He shall be remembered in the tales that come of this moment. For he is the one who told me how to find the shadow cat. He is the one whose words led me to you along with the crafty coral."

And with that, the jaguar faced northeast, put his paw forward, and turned his head to look into the eyes of Miracle.

"Ah," the child said, "I see you have found the way you need to go. The turtles have told you. Let us go, then!"

—m—

The friends passed by the fields of ostriches and emus, a vast plain of partitioned enclosures and open meadows. They came to a gate held by nothing more than a latch, which Miracle lifted for all of them to pass through. They turned due north.

"I was in this place before!" said Miracle. "I was here when Papá Eli and Tío Ubi helped me. I was here when Tío Sergio and the bad men tried to take me. This is where the birds with longs legs carried me from them!"

Some distance away on open terrain, a herd of ostriches eyed the friends with great caution.

"Well, would you look at that odd parade of creation!" said an ostrich. "There's a little Man among them, and I'll be a ballroom plume if it's not the very manchild who commandeered us eleven moons ago!"

"What do you mean?" said a younger ostrich. "I wasn't there then."

"No, I'll say you weren't," said the first one. "A good half the flock wasn't. Many who were there that day have passed into the great steel chute and not returned. But I'll tell you what happened, yes I will. That manchild threw his arm around the neck of old Archippus, the most introverted bird of our whole flock, an ostrich so to himself that he only spoke *once a week*! And that only in a whisper—as if he were a giraffe!"

"Yes, that's right!" another ostrich chimed in. "Archippus saved up everything he wanted to say for one moment every seven days. But he talked in his sleep when the moon was full. As his close friend, I should know."

"What happened with the manchild?" asked the younger ostrich.

"He climbed on his back," the first one said, "and rode him across the plain to a stable where that same horse and ring-tailed burglar were waiting for him! And see—How terribly strange!—the manchild walks with them *and* a dreaded meat eater while a falcon scouts the way!"

"A cheetah! A cheetah!" cried the younger ostrich.

"No, no, you fool!" rebuked the first, who craned his long neck forward and squinted. "The spots are different, the body too. He's stocky, not lithe, and his markings aren't just spots… they're spots *within* spots!"

And the ostriches, crowding together for fear, watched the strangers as they journeyed north.

"Behold, they go to the forbidden place!" the friend of Archippus said.

"Tell me why it's forbidden," asked the younger one. "I've never quite understood why it's such a big deal. It's been that way since I was a hatchling."

"It's forbidden because of that same manchild you're looking at!" the first one said. "He lorded it over us in that remote place they're heading to, and so we don't go near it. Not even the prince of Eden's Bend or his people go there. But it's not because they're afraid of it; it's because they're busy elsewhere. They haven't set to working on it yet. When they do, they'll tear the fence down and move it north to capture the new lands their hands have seized. But they haven't gotten 'round to that labor. That's why there's not a boot print or tire track for miles where they're going, just a whole lot of cactus and scrub cluttering the way, since we no longer trample it like we used to."

The younger one scratched the dust with his two-toed foot. "Pardon me, I know I've seen fewer summers than the rest of you, but didn't our fathers in the Maasai Mara teach us that Man is the rightful lord over us and can do with us as he pleases? It seems to me that a son of Adam riding Archippus elevates his glory—I mean both the glory of the ostrich and the glory of the manchild. Wouldn't you call it a noble thing that Archippus wielded the strength of his legs to carry the Namer? For sure it's nobler than jeering the Namer and outrunning him until he catches us for the chute and we disappear."

"Bite your tongue!" the first one said. "We don't talk about that here on Eden's Bend! Why do you think we stick our heads in the sand? It's to put off that unsavory business of—of submission. Ugh! Even the *word* tastes bad to say! You know the motto of the House of Struthio: 'Better to submit to dust than the Namer to trust!"

The friend of Archippus fanned his feathers. "Yes, whippersnapper, you should know better than to speak such nonsense!" And he bruised the young inquirer with a harsh peck to the neck. "To question our ways is to blemish our honor. Silence now, as we watch that parade of odd fellows disappear over the horizon and into their folly!"

—⚏—

The friends traversed disheveled ranks of scrub and cactus, picking their way through it as best they could, for there was no trail, only the kind of "path" created by places that had fewer thorns rather than many. The afternoon sun sapped their strength, but the thought of finding the answer to the quest kept their fatigue at bay.

Indeed, Patch thought, *the thirst of our bodies cheers on our thirst for discovery! 'Harmony of heart makes up for hardship!' as my uncle Milo used to say.*

After a time that seemed longer than it actually was—such is the work of avoiding thorns—they reached the northern border of Eden's Bend. Searching the fence line, they came upon the gate through which Miracle had escaped. There hung the bolt that had shut out El Dragón's men. The brass lock still remained open.

"Look!" said Miracle. "It is the door that helped me! This is the place where the running birds took me far from the bad men! Too far for them to chase me, too far for them to catch me. How good it is the birds took me, and how good it is the door was strong."

Miracle opened the gate. "You are free to find what you are looking for, my friends. After you. Go out with the word of the turtles. In Mérida, when Papá would go out, Mamá would kiss him and say, *'Que Dios te acompañe.'* I say that now to you."

And he kissed each one as they passed through the gate, even the Gulf Coast toad, as Miracle spoke Mamá's blessing.

"The weather just got milder," Bog said. "The touch of the child, the word of the child, the way of the child—his meekness does more than all the hot sun and humid air can muster. He makes them stand down without a shout. I surmise the boy's breathing air from the Garden we all long for in the Days of First Things. Somehow, for all the sorrow the boy's had to drink, there's still room in him for a river from another world where he can drink, too. Seems to me that there's still hope if a heart can still drink it."

The friends paused on the other side of the gate until Miracle led them. They crossed the gravel road where Papá Eli had contended with El Dragón's men. Before them was the dilapidated blacksmith shop half-hidden by tall stalks of pigweed and twisted trunks of steadfast ebony.

"The air is empty here," whispered Miracle, "as if the place has forgotten what happened that day. The iron poker still lies where it fell, the rod with a spear and a hook. The bad man hit Tío Ubi with it, but Tío knocked him down. No one has come here since then, or they would have moved the poker out of the way of feet and tires. The iron knows what happened, but no one has asked it to tell its story. We are safe from bad men for now."

Miracle turned to his friends. "Follow me!" He made his way through pigweed, the green and tiny blooms thereof clustered on stalks taller than his head, looming above him like spikes. A bobwhite darted from one with a seed in her beak. Another bobwhite followed her, clutching a berry, the fruit of an unseen shrub of saffron plum.

The friends followed Miracle and, once past the pigweed, found themselves in the remains of the blacksmith shop, its roof torn open and its sides bowed down by the seasonal blasts of wind, sun, and rain.

Bog croaked. "The preponderance of iron speaks here. It testifies to the sweat of Man and his hours of toil and labor. But it also testifies that that age of spark and fire and long gone. See how the bushes of the saffron plum grow up through fractured bricks that were once the floor. See how they flourish beneath the aging eaves. And see the signs of the deer who frequent here to delight in the saffron's sweet fruit, just like that bobwhite did—and just like that theona checkerspot butterfly does now. The deer, the bobwhite, the butterfly, and the saffron plum give equal testimony that in this place, Man's endeavors have fallen away."

Oracle stirred, his tale flowing parallel to his thoughts. "I have been here. I passed through this place in my search for the Lonely Tree."

Miracle saw the jaguar lift his head toward the ruin with eager eyes. "You know this place, good cat! I know it too. I stood here with Grandfather when Tío Sergio brought word of Mamá and Papá! It was a hard word in a hard place. Is this where the word of the turtles has sent you? Is their word hard too? I hope it is not like the word I heard." He walked among the saffron plum bushes and searched among them. "There is nothing here but the footprints of deer."

The theona checkerspot landed on his nose. Miracle became very still, shut his eyes, and listened to the touch of the butterfly.

"It tickles!" he giggled. The butterfly moved about the child's nose on delicate legs, each one awakening joy. The friends saw and wondered.

"She is speaking to me," Miracle whispered. "She says that the hard words I heard when I was here were only half the tale, for the end of a tale always knows laughter." He opened his eyes.

The checkerspot lifted off the child's nose, glided through the saffron plums and disappeared. Miracle followed her aerial trail. Beyond the bushes, he came upon a battered water trough hosting a pile of branding irons, which jutted out at haphazard angles. Their ends splayed into the air, some showing the branding end and some the handle. But one iron extended beyond the rest, and on that end it bore its symbol, a code for a sound from the lips of Men. There, on that midair sign, sat the checkerspot.

Miracle drew near. The checkerspot fluttered away, and the child stood face to face with the suspended riddle. He looked long at the form, cupping his head with one hand, and placing the other on his hip. "It is silent, but still speaking. It is waiting for me to give it a voice."

Oracle came and touched the branding iron with his nose. "What is this curious thing I have seen before when I passed through here? Is it what the coral and the turtles spoke of? It is not—and yet it is."

Patch squinted at the symbol so that the sign alone filled his eyes. "That ginormous snapper said, 'Turn it in your heart.'"

"How do we turn it that way?" asked Bog.

Plod uttered a neigh. "I've seen these in the hands of the vaqueros at their roundups. They place them in the fire till they glow. Then they place them on the new arrivals. The hot metal leaves a mark, like a hoofprint of sorts, the name of the manrealm the cattle belong to. It's a name burned in so deep that no one will forget it, or if they do, there's trouble. That's the way things are among Men and their realms."

Miracle looked at the symbol from one angle, then another. Suddenly, his eyes brightened. He picked up the iron and stamped the sign into the earth. And this is the mark it made: the manletter *B* set inside a diamond shape—the logo of Diamondback Ranch before the prince of Eden's Bend had acquired it.

"This is the sign I seek!" Oracle exclaimed. "When we turn it in our hearts it becomes so! Truly my eyes fell upon this iron code when I passed through a dozen moons ago, but it did not speak to me then, for I did not know the story it belonged to, nor did I turn it in my heart. But during my exile in the north, as I passed through the realm of the Brazos hermit, the coral snake drew me this sign to pass on to the turtles, for she knew it would prompt them to send us to it. The snapper guided us to it, and the manchild has given it a voice. It speaks of the final leg of our search. This is the place where we will find the trailhead to the shadow cat's hidden lair."

Patch searched the ground. "Here's a path the water uses when there's enough of her. I see the place where she's touched the earth."

He followed the dry sign of the stream through the debris of the derelict smithy. Though pigweed, broken bricks, and the bushes of the saffron plum hindered the view, the smooth lines of former waters never fully departed from sand and soil.

"This way!" he said. The friends followed him while Sent the falcon circled overhead.

The dry streambed reached a line of Rio Grande ash, whose roots spread boldly, then dove beneath the dirt. Beyond the tree line flourished more ash mingled with stands of sugar hackberry.

"These trees aren't as sun scorched as they should be," Plod commented. "There's water in the earth. I smell it."

"Yes, I smell it too," said Bog. "And what a savor it is! It reminds me of the time my late uncle Alfred fell out of a vaquero's haversack and had to cross the Tamaulipan Thorn Forest alone. Have I ever recited to you the Ballad of the Prickly Pear? One of those saved his life. If it hadn't been for a thornless patch where his fly-bare tongue could find succor, he would have perished before he reached the Rio Grande."

The horse whinnied softly. "I'm sure it's a good tale, but why don't we save it for after supper this evening?"

"You're right, Plod," the toad conceded. "A tale without good timing is like a poem without good rhyming!"

Patch did a double take. "Why, Bog, I've never heard you give way to Plod like that without a grumble!"

Bog replied with a long, low croak. "The journey has mellowed me, I suppose. Mind you, I still have the fight in me. You saw it with the snapper and you'll see it again if this streambed leads to danger. I won't back down if we're cornered. I'm from the House of Bufo, known for many heroic last stands. But I'm learning where to take a stand, and I'm learning where to stand down, for not every battle is do or die. And what would the tale of a life be like anyway if the trope was always the same: 'He got his way'? If I got my way every time, it would be a mighty boring tale, yes, monotonous enough to cause even the fireflies to dim their lights and slumber till it was over!"

The ash and the hackberry parted slightly before the travelers to reveal a purple sage in full bloom—the cenizo bush. And it was just at that same moment that the sound of running water reached them, a bubbling chuckle that called to the sage like an inside joke. The friends searched for the sound, and behold, there, winding through bushes of blooming cenizo, was a slender stream cool and clear!

Miracle bent down, cupped his hands, and brought the water to his lips. "Ah, the taste of smooth stones and sleeping rain!"

And the friends paused to drink.

Refreshed, they lifted their heads. Water poured off Oracle's whiskers as he rose. "The terrapins have been true to their word. Let us follow this stream to the home they promised would be at the wellspring." He nodded to Miracle, who nodded in return, and the child led, baptizing his feet in the stream as he walked.

The creek varied in depth from a coon's paw to a horse's hoof. Occasionally a clump of lantana or small mound of caliche broke the stream into two or three parts, but the waters always reunited again. And on either side, there was life: flowering stalks of the amaranth. Blooms of Drummond's onion. Mexican buckeyes with their three-lobed pods and black seeds scattered beneath them.

"The pods look like a game of marbles!" laughed Miracle. And, while the friends waited, he knelt on the ground and studied the arrangement of pods. He flicked one, and it struck two others, and they in turn careened into two pairs of pods, so that with one stroke the child caused seven to dance. He laughed as he rose, and all moved on.

The land flourished around them. Well-watered sunflowers bravely faced the sun, while beneath them grew silver-leaf nightshades with purple, star-shaped blooms and fruit like tiny tomatoes. Prairie coneflowers blossomed with petals swept back in joyful surrender to the sky, strengthened by the sweet water coursing through their stems, where healing properties awaited release. Such were the discoveries that unfolded as the friends followed the stream through a land given over to rest by a generation of abandonment from Man's labor-bound dreams.

Then came a slight rise of earth, where the waters chattered their way through a tumble of rock. Past a last hedge of cenizo, the stream spread out at its wellspring, a shallow pond broad enough for all the friends to stand in. And on the far side of the waters stood a great tepeguaje, some sixty feet tall, whose branches bore copious burdens of silver-white blooms and seed pods clustered in strips like worn leather. The roots of the tree stretched over the hillock and down among stones, but they parted in one place to reveal an opening: a small, silent cave.

Patch sniffed the air. "That opening's no wider than a badger or skunk would make, but there's no smell of either of those kinds. There's someone else in there…someone…new."

The friends rested in the waters, for the coolness imparted both strength and peace in such a way that they found the power to be still even on the edge of discovery. The falcon alighted on the tepeguaje, whose branches poured forth thick foliage almost touching the ground in a generous canopy of shade.

After a time, Miracle touched the jaguar's head. "Good cat, I think this is where you have something to do. Be blessed in it."

Oracle stepped forward and stood in the waters. A word stirred in him, and his tail stirred with it. The word moved from the depths of his heart through paths of his soul, drawing ever closer to where his tongue met the air. There, it took form, waiting for the Cat Who Remembers to give it a voice.

And here is how the word came: through a song. Oracle opened his mouth and sang it.

> *Man set me free to be the lord*
> *Of Valley long and winding*
> *To honor full the dying word*
> *Kahoo the Grave was binding*
>
> *The Valley cannot be complete*
> *Without a sense of mystery*
> *And you of all the cats I greet*
> *Are called into that history*

Miracle Gives the Iron a Voice

I summon now, I summon you
To come out of your hiding
I sing a song, I sing it true
An end to your time biding

And bring you to the light of day
To ply resacas' waters
As cats whose hunting looks like play
As cats who look like otters!

Oh jaguarundi, come to me
Out of the secret shadows
From cautious haunts to canter free
Among the mouse-rich meadows!

15

OUT FROM THE SHADOWS

In the darkness of the cave, a movement brushed past the lip of light spilling into the entrance. It was just enough for the friends to perceive fur. Beyond the light, shadows moved within the dark circle of the hole, the clarity thereof obscured by the blank, bright stare of the sun-bleached stones surrounding the entrance. A silent pause followed. Then a broad, blunt nose emerged, testing the outdoors for danger. The nose analyzed the air as the whiskers bowed back upon the edges of the hole before springing out once clear of it. Then both nose and whiskers took in the air, the sun, and the presence of those who had summoned him. The jaguarundi came out from the shadows.

His head was small, his forehead flattened, his facial features peculiar and fierce. His eyes, dark amber with a hint of jade, were close-set while his small ears were far apart. His elongated body was not unlike that of the otter, and his legs were short relative to his frame. Out his sleek form came, inch by inch, lithe and ready, muddy brown and charcoal gray: a fur the Maker had blessed the cat with such that the eye of Man did not covet it like he did the coat of his spotted cousins. Man had therefore left him in the shadows to do his assassin's work among the rodents of his realms. And though the jaguarundi was about a fourth of the jaguar's size and a fraction of his weight, he did not cower as he approached the great feline of the House of Panthera Onca. He halted at the jaguar's paws and nodded in honor without breaking his gaze.

"Sire, I am Myst the jaguarundi of the House of Herpailurus." He looked at Oracle with an intense stare.

Bog croaked. "You dare to stare down the lord of the Valley?"

The jaguarundi curled his tail around his body. "I have already stood before death and overcome the fear of that all-consuming gloom. Why should I fear who I see now?"

But Oracle said, "Welcome, Myst, Cat of Many Puzzles. I have finally met my match in staring. I defer to you."

"A shadow cat!" marveled Patch.

"A cat who was hiding!" exclaimed Miracle. "Is this the one Tío José said the farmers never saw? If it is, then it is el gato colorado—the cat who swims like an otter!"

Sent spread his wings in honor. "Their kind has been extinct in the Valley since the manyear 1986!"

"Not extinct, but hidden," Myst said, his eyes remaining on Oracle.

The lord of the Valley sat in the waters and looked deep into the shadow cat's amber-jade eyes. "Tell us your story."

The jaguarundi likewise sat in the stream as he beheld the tale before his mind's eye. "When Kahoo the Grave met his end at the hand of Man some seventy springs ago, we withdrew from the fellowship of the Three Tribes, for without a lord of the Valley, our ocelot and bobcat kin scattered while Man devoured our hunting grounds. We found no ears among them that would listen. So, we formed a secret society known only to the turtle—and to the coral snake, who swore on her colors to poison any who discovered us without the password from the terrapin tribes.

"With the trail of the jaguar empty, we retreated into the night, though we were made for the rising of the sun and the setting of the same. We retreated to the realm of rumor, where Man saw us in fleeting, unsure glimpses. We found refuge beneath the broad shade of this great leadtree, its bitter bark testifying to the taste of our tale. We who splashed in resacas cloistered in this cave, letting hope slumber, forbidding ourselves to be seen save in rumor form only. And so, we, the single surviving tribe of our near-extinguished house, hid our face from Man and beast—from all except our prey, that is.

"Our face has proven to be the last thing many a mouse and rat have seen on earth. With guard down and stomach full after gorging the farmer's field, the rodent tribes look up at the sky in sated satisfaction, only to find the face of the shadow cat emerge from the sheaves and bring about their sudden end.

"We have become the farmer's silent servant, invisible to Men of the soil, but whose trail of slain make them grin in gratitude. And so it is that the farmers of El Valle speak this proverb:

> *Greed of gut will slow you down*
> *When jaguarundi comes to town*
> *Self-denying feline kind*
> *Will overtake your lumb'ring hind*

But the season of seclusion has come to an end, for now before me is a cat of rosette spots, a cat of the House of Panthera Onca. A new lord of the Valley. We no longer need hide our face. Behold, I show it to you freely. You have my allegiance, sire." And the jaguarundi bowed with humble eyes.

Oracle received the shadow cat with a bow, then looked heavenward. His tail gently touched his side as he returned his gaze to the long-forgotten feline. "I rejoice that you have returned to the land of the seen, for you carry an irreplaceable paw. Your heart, your ways, and your story belong to your house only and cannot come to pass in the tribe of another. They can *share* in your story, but they cannot *become* it. What is more, I perceive the rule of the Valley is incomplete without you, for the jaguarundi imparts what cannot be found in the council of bobcat and ocelot alone. 'Pace' and 'Force' are not names only; they are signs of their natures and seals on their gifts. I foresee, therefore, that the courage of the House of Lynx Rufus and the cleverness of the House of Pardalis are incomplete without the mystery of the House of Herpailurus. That gift is yours, oh Myst of the Hidden Spring."

"Thank you, sire," Myst replied. "I am glad. I would never have emerged from the shadows if you had not returned first. But you have come. It is good you are here."

The two cats beheld one another. They added the savory herb of silence, strengthening the flavor of the discovery and deepening its joy. In the sacrament of that moment, a theona checkerspot butterfly landed in the space between them, resting on a stone. With each slow breath, she moved her wings back and forth as if to beckon the air to the gathering. The top side of her wings showed her signature pattern— orange, yellow, and black—while the underside of her wings revealed gentle stripes of orange and cream. The air grew clear, relieved somehow of the summer heat. In that cool interlude, Oracle kissed the butterfly with the tip of his nose. She fluttered and alighted on the stone again. The lord of the Valley lifted his head.

"Oh, how the hurricane of gulf waters harbored Kahoo's prayer! Oh, how the storm labored with the monarch butterfly to carry the Tale of the Last Jaguar to my ears in the heart of Sian Ka'an! Oh, how the fall of the monarch upon the limestone ruin became the wellspring of the stream that has led me here! My paws forged no trail, they only picked it up and moved it forward. And now I am here in the sojourn that will shift the season. It is a wonder to me, and more a wonder still when I consider how Man set me free to roam here after my capture. Why he did so, I do not know. But his choice, though ignorant of Kahoo's prophetic word, placed me perfectly for fulfilling it like a seed falling on fertile soil!"

Myst moved his tail back and forth above the waters. "You and I have in common Man's choice to set us free. Our tribe remembers it in the Tale of the Lonesome Echo. Long ago, in the manyear 1959, a seeker named Neill met our forefathers in the jungles of British Honduras, what Man now calls Belize."

"I have heard of that realm," Oracle said, "for the mangrove marshes and barrier reefs of my home extend into it."

"True," the shadow cat said, "as do the reptiles and amphibians the seeker named Neil befriended. He studied their ways and wrote them down on stacks of square leaves the color of ivory.

"When he departed for his home in the manrealm Florida, he took with him a male and female of our kind. Blaze and Bella were their names. At the Suwanee River near the manplace called Chiefland, he released them. They prospered. They met a diaspora of their kin who had preceded them on the ships of Man as he traded between nations, some jaguarundis arriving as stowaways and some as caged passengers who eluded their captors after landfall. The scattered ones gathered to the pair Neill released. He released more, and these, too, came under the leadership of the first pair. They became a great ruling house for length of days and extended the territory of our tribe. Their descendants can be found as far as the realms of Mississippi and Alabama. One family even set out as far as the stream-fed hills in the heart of Texas, so the sparrows tell us as they relay their chirping tales from tree to tree and realm to realm. They say they prospered there too.

"But here in the Valley, it has been different. We have hidden ourselves. No one commanded us to prosper like Neill of Chiefland. Therefore, our story in the Valley has fallen into forgetfulness. It turned from a story of remembering to a story of waiting. But now that you are here, we no longer wait."

Oracle breathed a satisfying sigh. And in the pause that followed, Miracle waded a few steps until he was beside him. He rested his hand on the cat's back. Oracle looked at him, accepting the scratch on the head he gave him, then turned again to the jaguarundi.

"The touch of the manchild reminds me of his many unnamed elders who rule this realm. The mystery of Man's Three Choices awaits me yet again. For though one Man set me free, another Man may take me from the earth or bind me again behind glass panes and iron bars. You know that I may not be here long, oh Cat of Many Rumors."

Myst lifted a paw. "So you say, but your coming will be enough to keep us from going into hiding again, even if you depart. Be at peace, sire. You have found us, and we shall not go into hiding again. Remembering you shall be sufficient food for our journey under the sun, upon the waters, and with the glow of the midnight moon."

Oracle gave the call of his kind. "I am glad, for if you rejoin the Cats of the Three Tribes, they can rule a restored animal kingdom, renewed in life and honor. A final spring where they will not only be caretakers, but pathmakers."

The jaguarundi purred. "Such a future would enrich our lives more than a meadow full of mice. For the flesh of the field comes and goes, but this story of your coming and a final spring is food that remains and keeps imparting, be the field empty or full."

Oracle rose, the fresh waters of the spring running in rivulets down his fur. He shook, christening the cat, the friends, and the tepeguaje. "Even so, oh shadow cat, it is better that you remember not only this story, and not only your stories of journey and exile, but also the *first* story, the one belonging to you alone, when the Namer's eyes discovered your kind and spoke. Come close, that you might remember your name."

Myst did so, bringing his forehead to rest beneath the mouth of the lord of the Valley. And the shadow cat received the Breath of Remembrance. When he stepped back and raised his head, his eyes glowed like one who has discovered the hiding place in the house where an ancestor had hidden the inheritance. The shadow cat made a series of birdlike chirps and whistles—two of his tribe's thirteen calls. And from within the cave and behind the foliage came a stirring of paws in motion. Then the air filled with purrs and yaps and the chattering of young. The jaguarundi had returned to the Valley.

16

AT HOME UNDER THE STARS

Tío José and Tía Lourdes spoke almost no words while waiting for Paco that afternoon. For the better part of those creeping hours, the exchange between them was nothing more than an occasional inquiring look from the one and an assuring nod from the other. Both waited for the sun to reach that time when the gloaming of the sky called all things to gather with their kinds, and, in the waiting for that moment, each chose a different way to redeem their restlessness. Tía Lourdes busied herself with searching her kitchen for the matching lid of every container, which, much like socks, seemed to wander away from their mate on their own. Tío José watered his pumpkins and sunflowers, bending at the base of each plant to pour life-giving liquid from a slowly flowing hose. But the task took much longer than it should have, for every few minutes he would rise and face east, and there he would stand, as still as a fortress sentinel, seeking the earliest possible glimpse of the boy's return. When he finished watering the garden, he opened a bottle of cold water from the cooler Tía Lourdes had stocked and placed by the folding chairs. He kept watch. Before him stretched the empty plain to the eastern horizon. The smell of fresh cooked fish bathed in savory herbs reached him from inside the trailer.

Tía Lourdes appeared at the screen door. "Dinner's almost ready."

Her husband nodded. "Then he will be coming soon."

"Are you sure?"

"I am sure."

"What if something has happened?"

He grinned. "I am sure something has happened, mi querida, but that will not prevent our son from coming home. It will only give him a story to tell."

"I'm putting the plates on the table."

"Go ahead. I will ride out to the tree line."

Riding the palomino, Tío José arrived at the edge of the anacua trees. Behind him was the field of hay bales. On his right, far to the south, he watched a group of vaqueros getting into their vehicles, their day's work done on Eden's Bend. Some were departing the ranch for vacation, for it was the Saturday before the Fourth of July, and they had earned the whole coming week off. Others drove toward the company cafeteria, the smoke of whose barbecue pit wafted in a thin cloud above the roof. A few others made their way toward the trailer park.

Footsteps sounded on the forest floor. At a place where scattered straw met trees, the friends emerged from among the branches: Paco, the horse, the toad, the raccoon, the jaguar, and a strange animal that looked too feline to be a weasel but too otter-like to be a bobcat. The falcon flew above them in a wide, slow arc.

"You left with four, but you have come back with five!" exclaimed Tío José. "I have not seen such a gathering of six in all my life!"

Paco laughed. "No, Tío, we are seven! You forget the toad rides in the horse's hair! They are lifelong friends and my friends too."

As the horse grazed on blades of grass among the straw, Tío José saw the mottled skin of the Gulf Coast toad nestled inside the mane. The toad held on to the horse's ear to remain aloft as the horse stooped his great head.

"Ah, yes, the toad in the horse's mane. How could I forget! He sang an old song on our way here from the barn, if I understood him right. And of course I shouldn't expect him to hop all afternoon with so many feet and hooves to dodge. If I were an old toad, I would save my strength and my hide that way too."

Paco hugged Plod's neck and spoke into his ear. "You who carried me everywhere, I will remember *you* everywhere! You and the friend in your mane who sang us to sleep every night!"

He petted Bog on the head. "You have many new songs to sing because of today!"

Tío José's eyes turned to the jaguarundi, who rolled on his side to stretch his limbs while his body arched in a sharp curve. "And who is this—this one who has come out with you?"

"This is the friend the good cat was looking for. We asked the turtles for help, and they told us where to find him. I helped too, and we found him in a little cave by a secret freshwater spring."

The child gaped in surprise at a new thought. "Tío! I have found a freshwater spring too, just like you! You found the secret in salty water, but I found it on salty land! We both know a secret!"

Tío José dismounted and squatted before the jaguarundi, looking at him intensely. "Son, you have found two secrets, not one! You found a hidden spring, but you also found a hidden cat. This is *el gato colorado*! It must be. The farmers' words from childhood bear witness to what I see!"

The jaguarundi flopped to his other side for a moment, sat up, and cleaned a paw.

The boy came to him. "Goodbye, secret cat. I'm glad I helped find you."

And the shadow cat bowed to the manchild.

Paco turned to Oracle. The jaguar sat sphinxlike in calm confidence while the child scratched the back of his head. The cat leaned into the pleasure of it as Paco spoke.

"Thank you, good cat, for asking me to tell you my story. I'm glad I have been a help to you today. I will go now. I promised Tía I would be home by supper. Farewell, good cat! ¡Adios! I will see you again!"

He hugged the jaguar, who flicked the boy's cheek with his tongue. They were still for a moment in a thoughtful embrace.

Paco knelt and looked into the eyes of Patch. He put his arms around the raccoon and buried his face in the fur. Then Patch nuzzled the boy's face. The child smiled through eyes brimming with tears. "Thank you, my marble-loving friend. Thank you for the treasures, the tea, the food…Thank you for everything!"

Tío José did not realize that his mouth had been open the whole time until he noticed how dry his tongue was. He swallowed with difficulty and wiped the back of his hand across forehead and eyes, mixing sweat and tears of his own.

The animals were all looking at him now, at rest and watchful, the light in their eyes one of placid expectation.

"So, it falls to me again," the vaquero said. "I can tell by their way. But this time there is joy in the tears running down my cheek, not sorrow. Potrillo, take my hand."

He gently hoisted the boy onto the saddle at the horn. Paco waved to his friends. "¡Gracias!"

Tío José tipped his hat to the animals, a look of embarrassment on his face. He tried to speak, but found his throat had choked up. He tried again, this time taking his hat fully off. "*Que Dios te bendiga, muchachos.* Until we meet again."

And with that, the manchild the birds named Miracle departed. The friends watched until he was lost in the shivering air dancing at the horizon beyond the bales of hay on the distant, barren plain.

Patch's nose throbbed. He drew his paws over it, sliding them down several times until the sniffling had come to rest. "He knew the language of the marbles. We spoke to each other through them. All of mine are with him now. I'm full knowing he will take care of them, but empty knowing I may never see him again. I still have my treasure pouch at the eucalyptus, and I can always find new marbles, but to find a friend, that is a much harder thing."

Oracle rubbed the side of his head along the raccoon's fur. "Miracle remains a friend even if he is not on the trail with us. We do not know where his trail leads, whether it forks away or comes back to meet our own. But it may, Fair Bandit, it may. The only way to know is to keep walking the trail given us. Then we will see if the child's trail joins ours again. Then we will know."

Plod gave a gentle neigh. "But in the meantime, the manchild is on his own trail, for he must be with his kind. He's got a few more tears to shed, I reckon, in front of that marker for his parents. Things like that don't just have one cry in 'em. That's how it was with my own ma and pa when they departed for the Wide Green Fields. I figure it's the same for the manchild."

"Yes," Oracle said, "he must mourn the loss of his parents, and he must learn the ways of his new family. He must grow in his body too, for the journey in the wilderness was hard on his frame, but now that he is healed of it, he will grow like a tree planted by living streams."

Patch dried his eyes with his paws and sighed. "Well, sire, I guess it's time for us to pick up the trail again. It's the same one you've been following from the time I met you at Garfight Pond clear up to Firefly Lake last night!"

"Yes, Fair Bandit, it is time to continue our own sojourn, time to make pilgrimage to the place of the cats' own choosing, the place the bobcat and the ocelot will decide: a Council of the Cats, where our jaguarundi companion here will be revealed and the stewards of the Valley restored as the Three. I await word from the green jay as to where that shall be. And after that, if Man's Three Choices do not corner me first, there shall be a Court of the Animals."

Bog crooned a long note. "A Court and a Council! The stuff of ancient songs. And you mean to add more stanzas to those songs, oh Cat Who Remembers."

Oracle rose, his tale lithe with readiness. "Yes, I do. If I can achieve this quest, the animal kingdom of the Valley will see a final season of abundant life, abundant freedom, and abundant honor. A final spring."

Plod shook his mane to shoo off a horsefly. "And if Man blocks your trail?"

Oracle lowered his tail to the ground. "If Man blocks my trail, then no more springs. No new season in the Valley. Only a halfhearted winter until the Morning Star rises at the end of days. This is how it shall be for the animal kingdom if I do not complete my journey 'from here to river's end,' as Kahoo prayed."

Patch reflected on these things, and, though he did not mean to, his thoughts ran in two directions at once.

Oracle sounds like he's saying goodbye when he's just getting started! I'd better make the most of every living minute I've got with my friend! I'd better do my part. But my treasure pouch at the eucalyptus! Talking about it just now—and last night at Firefly Lake—really gets me missing my treasures. If Oracle's quest fails, what will become of them? Miracle will take care of my marbles, but what about the rest? Oh, me! Half my heart is courageous with things greater than a paw can hold, and the other half is preoccupied with my own petty collections!

Patch cornered his thoughts and turned them into a question. "Oracle, what about the trees? Does your quest help them too?"

The jaguar looked at the anacua branches. "As goes the animal kingdom, so goes the plant kingdom. To speak of the one is to include the other. They go together. Yes, my quest also serves the trees."

"And what about the special things the trees keep?"

"Special things? Do you mean the memories they carry and the stories they tell?"

"Ah, yes, yes, of course, those things…but other things too, like newborn cubs and hatchlings and…well, collections of treasures from the Borrows that the House of Procyon goes on from time to time. What about *those* special things?"

Oracle smiled. "When a river flows, all plants drink and all roots benefit. It is the same with all special things when the kingdom is restored, your collections included. If the quest succeeds, there will be abundance, enough for every animal to flourish under his own Mustang vine and eucalyptus tree. But if the quest fails, we will remain a realm of survivors and scavengers…So rise, let us go before the worried eyes of Man chance upon us."

Patch scanned the horizon for stray vaqueros. "Good idea, sire, but I'm curious: Why didn't Miracle's new uncle raise a fire rod against you? His eyes were anxious like all Men's are, and yet he accepted us after the first fright fell from him. He was still."

"It was the boy's peace that stilled him. And ours. You, the child, and our company of feather, fur, hoof, and hide helped him remember his name."

The friends journeyed by way of the thickets until nightfall, where they found a clearing not far from the beach. A group of dunes rose amid bluestem and railroad vines. The dunes made a natural defense, being slightly higher than the ground around them, and yet in their center was a hollowed-out place, lower than the dunes, providing shelter.

A bird call sounded, a muttered buzz of a quack that seemed to pass on secrets stumbled upon at bayou bottom. The spoonbill stood on the crest of a dune. He raised his wings in the shape of a wide letter *M*, lowered his head, and swung it in greeting.

Sent the falcon landed beside him, tapped his beak, and turned to the friends. "With the arrival of my fellow flock member, I shall go now. If it weren't for two things we see, one glorious and one ominous, I would have said that the Colony of the Lost had fulfilled what it had decided to do, for we have kept watch until the child has returned to the family of Man. But we see a glorious thing in that Miracle has not just found a house; he has found a *home*. And we should linger over such a place, for today I saw how the uncle who cares for the child is, himself, a child at heart, trusting one step ahead of his understanding when goodness, truth, and beauty bear witness to that trust. Likewise is the heart of his better half, the aunt who is strong in speech but meek before mysteries. What is more, it is clear to us the manchild will remain with his new aunt and uncle as more than a guest, for we see the rulers of Man meeting with them often, and the air grows bright around their manplace."

"It sure *does* grow bright!" Patch said. "Bright enough for the aunt and the uncle to let us rest in the shade of their dwelling while the manchild plays. It's as much a safe place for us as it is for Miracle. Our job is done."

The falcon hunched his shoulders for a moment as he lifted and refolded his wings. "Yes, Patch, the air is bright. But, as I said, there is also an ominous thing which moves the Colony of the Lost to remain at watch, for we perceive that Miracle is only safe for a season. There are shadows in the distance regarding the manchild, a restless darkness. And the distance from that darkness narrows day by day."

The falcon bowed toward Oracle. "Therefore, in light of these things both glorious and ominous, we, the Colony of the Lost, rejoice to remain. We will serve your quest, oh Lord of the Valley, you and your fellow sojourners. For the shadow cat has been found. Forgotten things have been remembered. New things are in store. We delight to keep watch. I leave you in the care of my odd-beaked fellow. It is his turn among us to abide with you. Farewell."

The friends watched the falcon depart, leaving behind him no path but a clear sky bathed in constellations. The spoonbill foraged out a stray sliver of cypress bark from among his feathers before he flapped his wings until they coaxed the air to carry him.

The moon peeked above the waters of the Laguna Madre as the spoonbill flew above the dunes in a slow, ascending spiral. And when he was high enough to see both the moonlight on the waters and the friends below, he gave the call of his kind. A breeze from the sea washed over the land.

One by one, the friends reclined, first the jaguar, then the raccoon, then the jaguarundi, resting with their sides touching one another.

Plod looked at them. He flapped his lips as he exhaled and drew a gentle hoof across the earth. "Well, this sand-dune stable with strange bedfellows is not how things normally are, but maybe it's how things used to be, back when we all remembered our names."

"Fascinating!" Bog whispered to Plod as he clung to his ear. "There is no war here as there often is between things of unlike kind. No last stand. Only rest and fellowship with the dunes for our defense. Maybe this is not only how things used to be, Plod. Maybe this is how things will be again. I think it's worth risking my hide to find out. Come, old friend, you're weary. Let's recline too. If they turn on us while we sleep, it won't be because we picked a fight. If it turns out that we don't see morning light, it won't be because we were afraid to hope. Take courage. Let's hope. Lie down and rest."

And so Plod did, bringing Bog with him. The great back of the horse joined the collective mound of fur, all claws at rest, all teeth asleep, all hearts facing the future with the same confident surrender of a beach facing a sea. No one growled, no one grumbled, but all made room to welcome the beast of burden unburdened from his fears. A cadence of breathing ensued, along with the shadow cat's purring.

The spoonbill saw. He threw his beak toward the moon, who affirmed the bird's wonder with a beatific glow while Jupiter, Saturn, and Mars bore witness to the joy.

And, bathing in that joy, a song came to him. He sang as Salt the owl had sung while he flew above Miracle as the boy, in the company of the friends, wound his way through the palo verde forest. But spoonbills do not sing in three-quarter time as owls do; they sing in four-four. Here is what he sang. The dew heard it as she passed by and preserved it in her drops, imparting the song to everything she rested upon that night.

Waters rising, waters falling
Dew descending, memories calling
From the shadows out of hiding
Come the mysteries still abiding

Now together, now a-traveling
Through the woven world unraveling
Pillars totter till their tumbling
Yet a new thing won't stop rumbling

From between the sleeping sand dunes
Speaks its coming like the stone runes
On forgotten boulders showing
One got here before you knowing

And did lay the new foundation
For a born-again creation
Where the jaguarundi slumbers
(Among friends the raccoon numbers)

And a jaguar doesn't wrestle
With the horse and toad who nestle
Their warm breathing backs beside him
Seven springtimes shall betide them!

Eden's echo now has spoken
And the boy becomes a token
Of a friendship soon returning
To a weary earth still yearning

That the drought of hope is ending
And the arc of time yet bending
To reveal all that is hidden
Until children run through Eden!

The friends listened with attentive ears, though their eyes were closed. The words descended into the hearts of the listeners and to the *yes* that waited for them there.

Oracle lay in a semi-curved position with his chin curving over his paws. His body was flatter than one may have expected, for cats have quite flexible joints in their bones, and when they rest, their frame allows for them to spread upon the ground.

Myst lay on the jaguar's right. The shadow cat's nose rested between his paws, his whiskers touching the quiet face of Oracle.

Leaning on the jaguar's other side was Patch, who faced away and toward the jaguar's tail. Patch had firmly lodged his back into the frame of his great friend. (*There's never been a tree hollow more secure than this place!*) The raccoon's bushy-ringed tail, attached as it was to the dreams of Fair Bandit, occasionally moved, tickling the great cat's ears, which twitched on their own in response to the teasing without stirring Oracle from his journey into slumber.

Plod, his legs folded beneath him, rested beside the raccoon.

On the ground beside Plod was Bog. After singing an ode to his ancestors who had fallen in the Great War of the Swamp Fire, he decided to hop into the mane of his equine friend.

The Gulf Coast toad whispered into the drowsy horse's ear, "It's out of foresight I do this, not out of fear of being eaten. For, the rest here is so complete, and the sleep so deep, that you or one of our companions might roll over in the night and squash me unawares. That would be an ignoble end." Thus, with a clear conscience that he was not cowardly but prudent, Bog reclined on the secure height of the back of the beast of burden.

And there, soothed by the lullaby of the whispering shore, all the friends fell asleep one by one, at home under the stars with no barred cage to mock them, no moat to block their way, no ironthorn or firestring to afflict them, but a foretaste of a time to come when the Gardener of Eden would finish the work begun long, long ago in the time when all remembered their names.

17

THE JABBER OF JAYS

The lord of the Valley has returned!"
Gem the green jay proclaimed her news from tree to tree the night she met the jaguar Oracle. The live oak and the willow saw her dart through their branches. The yaupon and the yucca watched her flash past their blades. The mesquite and sweet acacia, drowsing in the drought, awakened to the rush of her green feathers.

"The lord of the Valley has returned!"

Javelinas grazing among agaves looked up; screech owls perched in their hollows looked down; and the horned lizard clinging to the creosote paused to wonder. And on she flew.

The next day, as Oracle, Miracle, and the friends searched Bear Claw Ranch for the hidden lair of the shadow cat, Gem continued southward across the vast ranch of Eden's Bend with her message. As she announced the arrival of the lord of the Valley to a herd of cattle known as American Red, the cattle egrets accompanying them lifted en masse and flew in a circle around her.

"We've seen him! Yep, sure for shootin' have!" a cattle egret said. "The Rio Grande ground squirrels passed the word to us yesterday! By sunset members of our flock had flown north and found him. Now we're each taking turns going up for a look-see. We're mighty proud of that accomplishment.

Takes some pretty big news to get us doing flyovers when there's so much work to do plucking ticks off this herd!"

"Your word spurs me on," Gem replied. "Something new and beautiful has come to the Valley!"

Gem ate little, drank wherever a pond remained, and rested only enough to regain her strength against the wind, which, though invisible, made its presence vivid. Treetops swirled as if they were mopheads plunging into the buckets of giants scrubbing the sky. The wind increased its resistance against her, at times pushing her aside, at times meeting her head-on. She flew higher; the wind was there. She flew into a thicket; the wind was there. She flew low, but the wind forced her flight even more groundward, hindering her wings.

Gem crossed the fence line of Tripp's realm. She navigated neighboring Laguna Atascosa, which Man had set apart to remain wild. On hearing her message there, plovers raised their heads, Texas tortoises pondered the news, and peregrine falcons perched in pensive silence. But it was the great kiskadees who spoke. With bright yellow bodies and copper-colored wings, the birds formed a fluttering cloud.

"We've seen him!" said one, her beaming face bearing a bold stripe of black on white. "The deer-mice told us, and just now one of our own has returned to confirm it. And she's a different bird than she was this morning, I say. Same feathers, but new song. She breathed an air that's moving among us now, the Breath of Remembrance! Adam's word!"

On Gem flew through manplaces bristling with lights, billboards, water tanks, and cell phone towers, where things both wild and tame abided within wary reach of each other.

It was night again when Gem found an oak-filled park aglow with the lights of Man but empty of his presence. Here she came upon a flock of her cousins, the brown jays. They rested on a dozen branches, heads bowed within their wings or cocked to one side with eyes closed as the wind rocked their resting places in the same way choppy waters bob an anchored skiff. Their wings were shades of sugarless coffee, their breast feathers the off-white of condensed milk.

"Why have you awakened us?" a brown jay asked.

"Because this news cannot wait until you wake yourself. A jaguar has returned to rule the animal kingdom, a thing that has not been for seventy springs. The lord of the Valley has returned!"

"Are you an eyewitness?" asked one brown jay.

"Yes, I am! What I say is true!"

"Be that as it may, why bother us about it?" complained one brown jay. "How will his return change anything in our world for good?"

Gem sang the call of her kind in reply. "It could refresh the waters. It could revive the trees. It could restore the paths of the four-footed ones. Your feathers could be fuller because of it."

"But will they be *safer*?" asked another brown jay, rubbing the sleep from his eyes with a wing.

"That I do not know."

"Will the jaguar deal with the coyotes?" another asked in a tone of annoyance.

"I do not know."

"What about that brutish bobcat and secretive ocelot?" asked another, more annoyed than the one before.

"He is their ruling cousin," Gem reasoned. "Your nests will be farther from the reach of unlawful paws. When you build them, they will rest firmer in the boughs."

"But when we build them, will they be *easier* to build?" contested the brown jay. "And when we build them, will they *surely* be out of harm's way? Unlawful paws, yes, but what about *lawful* ones?"

"I do not know that either," Gem said with exasperation. "There is the wind and there is the wilderness. We still live tangled in the laws of both of those. I cannot predict where the wind will blow any more than I can explain where it comes from, and I cannot foretell what the wilderness will do on any given dawn, whether it will hold back harm or send it."

"There sure seems to be a lot more you *don't* know than you *do* know!" jeered a brown jay.

"Yes," Gem agreed, "but what I do know makes my wings light, my beak strong, and my flight a delight in the face of the wind. That is enough for me. You know what we jays say: 'It's the berries on the tree, not the roots you can't see, that give the branch its name.'"

"Well, yes, so we do say," an older brown jay said. "That is the wisdom of the House of Corvidae. The fruit tells us if the tree is good or bad for us jays. The hackberry bears one fruit, the persimmon another, and both are good for us in their season. But the soapberry is another story."

The brown jays hushed as the air filled with the sound of another flock arriving. The call of the new birds was like a cloud of airborne alarm clocks, brief refrains of clear notes or click-like buzzes, which, had they been on an actual clock, would have begged a response from the sleeper to press "snooze" or get out of bed.

The green jays appeared. They landed in the oaks and turned their heads like one turns his head when pushing open a door with the shoulders. And though the shape of their bodies was similar to their brown jay cousins, their markings, like Gem's, were a startling contrast. Bright blue hooded the head, spilling back from the beak and blending with a black smock pouring down the chest like an inkblot spread to its limits. Together both made a pattern—a dash of blue above each eye immersed in black; a splash of blue invading the dark's domain—so that the face of the green jay presented an intrepid, even audacious, disposition. Clothing the birds were green feathers dusted with aqua-tinged plumes while a yellow hue, dusted with green, covered the breast.

The flock dispersed among a dozen branches opposite the browns, adorning the trees as if they were gourds of solid fruit or precious stones whose colors still spoke despite the night's attempt at hushing them. Therefore, even before they opened their beaks, they dominated the browns. For though the coffee color of the one flock might remind one of that which wakes the body, it is the emerald, sapphire, and sable hues of the other that awaken the soul.

"What have we here?" asked a green jay. "A jabber of jays and we aren't invited? We will have none of this. If the browns are present, the greens will be too! Our blue- and gray-winged cousins are exempted, for their homes are too far north. But *we* would like to know if our feathers will be ruffled or smoothed by your news, for, one way or the other, it will touch us. What is your message, Gem?"

She hopped to the end of an oak bough stretching roughly toward the center of the jabber of jays. With the clarion call of a chortling jay, she announced the news. "A jaguar has returned to rule the animal kingdom of the Valley. His name is Oracle of Sian Ka'an. He will hold a Council of the Cats at the place of their choosing. I'm on my way to tell the chief ocelot and chief bobcat, the ones named Pace and Force. Once they decide on the place of the council, I will inform the lord of the Valley, who awaits in the manrealm known as Eden's Bend. He will go to the cats first in council. Then, in the Sanctuary of Sabal Palms, he will summon the animal kingdom for a Court of the Animals. Such a thing has not happened since Man took up the jaguar from the Valley seventy springs ago. This is a new thing!"

The green jays and brown jays took in the news in a variety of ways. Some released a whirr of sounds that seemed a cross between a whistle and the clicker that sheep herders use with their sheepdogs. Some sounded off staccato calls. Others reacted by whispering behind raised wings or murmuring furtively. And some turned their backs on Gem, leaning toward each other with intense whispers eye to eye, the tension of their thoughts revealed by their tails jerking like staplers above trembling paper. Each thought became bound to a fear, so that the strength was not in the thoughts themselves, but in the power that bound them.

A green jay spoke loud enough for all to hear and quiet the rest down. "Why did you not sound the alarm of our kind when you saw him?"

Gem cocked her head in thought as she recalled the moment on the palo verde branch from which she spied him below. "Well, for one thing, the jaguar had not seen me. Although I was close enough for his tail to brush the bottom of my branch, the foliage hid me. That gave me time to consider what to do."

"But what else could you do?" a green jay replied. "Alarms are second nature to us, and our cry not only helps *us* escape danger, but other tribes too when they hear our cries."

Gem chirped in agreement. "I know it's our second nature, but I don't know why I held back. Maybe it's because I was so surprised. Jaguars have not roamed South Texas since the days of the clear-cutting vaqueros. True, jaguars are spoken of in the tales at our flock's gatherings during the hour of dusk, and we mention him in 'The Quest of Amberjade,' our renowned ancestor who traveled from one pole to pole in search of where songs come from. But no one, no one as far back as any of us can remember, has ever actually seen one until now. Perhaps that's why I didn't sound the alarm: it was too good to be true."

"Or too *bad* to be true," retorted a brown jay.

"Point well taken," Gem buzzed back. "I wasn't sure which at first either. I guess that's why I hesitated. Fear and delight were both at work in me, and it wasn't clear which should prevail."

"I doubt the delight part," a green jay jeered.

Gem whistled as she worked her wings. "Well, if it wasn't delight, it was certainly something good. Maybe the word *awe* fits the beak better to describe what I felt. He was so big that a *dozen* of us jays could have perched on his back."

"Yes, and with a flick of his tail, we'd all be struck down!" cried a brown jay.

"I agree with my cousin," a green jay rattled. "The ocelots are no match for such a cat. It would take a dozen of *them* to match him in combat, and there haven't been that many ocelots in one place in the Valley since the mantribe of the Spanish sought their pelts!"

"What are you talking about, you feather-head green?" snapped a brown jay who was mostly gray. "Ocelots steer clear of jaguars. We've seen that in the forests of El Cielo in Tamaulipas. If there's a jaguar here in the Valley, the ocelots certainly won't contend with him and certainly won't welcome him! They'll flee and look after their own fur. We can expect no help from them. We're on our own when it comes to protecting our broods."

Gem made a raspy call as she began her rebuttal. "What you say would be true if the jaguar were after our nests. He would be a much greater threat than the bobcat and the ocelot. But it was not great weight and size that struck me with awe only; there was a quiet confidence about him that was weightier than the body itself. His was not the spirit of a thief, skulking in stealth to steal our broods. His was the spirit of someone who truly *owned* what he possessed. He was in no hurry. He was not poised to pounce or crouched to flee. He simply *was*."

With that last word, Gem returned to silence. The greens and the browns quietly consulted one another. Then a brown spoke:

"If the jaguar's arrival helps us survive, then we are for it. But mind you this: We will keep our distance while it unfolds. We will observe from the trees, but we will not give our feathers to it. For we brown jays have learned to adapt and endure through quiet reservation. Yes, since the departure of the last jaguar seventy springs ago, our tribe has accepted the tradition of silent watchfulness as the coat that suits us.

"True, there was a time when we were the most talkative of the jays, even more than the whiskeyjack, our distant kin who can't stop chatting about his trivial daily 'discoveries.' But through trial and sorrow, we have learned that, to avoid more trials than our breasts can bear, we must keep our heads *down*. We must guard our hearts. We must 'hunker or hunger,' as the brown jay saying goes. 'For safety to hold sway, keep out of harm's way!' And many another proverb like these do we drop into the ears of our broods while we drop worms into their beaks. Only with such wisdom is there hope for a brighter day. Not for us, most likely, for our days may end with little more than a whimper, but perhaps for some distant generation. That's the best we can do."

A green jay hopped onto the branch where Gem was and gave a shrill cry. "We greens, on the other hand, take a much different approach: Question everything. Make noise about everything. This becomes our armor. This becomes our friend. For you see—though it's true we ourselves can't keep track of all we're saying—to create a cloud of words is the same as hiding among the trees. It gives us time to see from the safety of not being seen. It gives us time to decide what to do. It gives us time to succeed, and succeed we will, for, as our brown jay cousins have said—one must do what one must do to adapt, endure, and survive. And for us greens, survival is through pecking and scratching our way out of each jabbering jam. Yes, this way there may be a brighter day ahead. Not for us, most likely, for our days may end with little more than sound and fury, but for some distant generation, perhaps. For some distant day." And the green jay returned to his perch.

Gem let out a call of exasperation and flew in a tight circle before the gathering in the oaks around her. She alighted again on the central bough, where, methodically, she looked at each jay as she turned on the branch, staring all down into silence. Her glance gleamed with cheer and a choice as fixed as sunlight on steel, her eyes made all the clearer in their intent by the contrasting black about them.

"But if you had seen what I had seen, you would be neither hiding nor howling. You would be silent but your heart would brim with joy. You would speak but hold back the best part for yourself and your Maker. You would be willing to risk but cautious to approach. He is beautiful, this jaguar, beautiful, I say! And though I don't have a good explanation for it, the jaguar's beauty disarmed me and itself became the explanation. A confidence deeper than words. A fear too embracing to reject. Before I knew it, the jaguar's beauty had made a nest in me, and now I am burdened with it. It is a burden I gladly bear. A burden that gives me wings!"

The greens and the browns began to all talk at once, one to another, for a fresh breath had swept through them, breathing life into each warble, click, call, and whirr.

Gem, emboldened by their response, was about to speak even more freely, when, at that moment, a manmachine came growling into the park. All the jays became instantly still. Their forms blended with the riddled shadows of the trees, making them perfectly invisible to the event below, which was so close that the aroma of both Man and machine filled their senses. This is what they saw:

18

THE WILL OF GEM

A chrome-blue 1973 Chevrolet Monte Carlo crept beneath the branches on silver-spoked wheels giving off a rhythmic glint in their orbit. The Monte Carlo stopped beneath an oak, cloaked in the darkness the branches gave. After a pause just long enough for the wind to jostle the trees, a chrome-violet 1977 Chevrolet Impala arrived, its hubcaps bearing curved blades flickering as they turned. The Impala's body was so low to the ground that, had it been equipped with a sense of smell, it would have tracked the path it prowled like the predators that hunted its namesake. The Impala rolled to a halt in the shadows.

The first ones to exit the Monte Carlo caused every last jay to bend their knees in preparation to flee in frantic flight, for the feet that touched the well-worn grass were not human. Two Komodo dragons dropped to the ground, each bound by a rhinestone collar to a leather leash disappearing into the car. The Komodos' tongues tasted the air. Their eyes searched the darkness. Next, in shoes made of leather from a reptile cousin of those same pets, out stepped a Man. The leashes converged about the fist of their master and wound into one twisted braid.

The Man wore a simple, functional suit with no adornment on wrists, neck, or fingers, save a single gold ring bearing the face of a roaring lion. A garnet filled the mouth; obsidian covered the eyes. As for the face of the Man, it bore a look as immovable as that of a statue, which remains in one disposition through every season. There was no fear on his face, but there was no courage either. It was the look of one who had died to hope long ago, but who was determined to not die alone.

From the Impala came Izzi and Sergio. Izzi spoke.

"Greetings, Señor Dragón. You are kind to meet us."

"It is not kindness that brings me here," El Dragón replied. "It is the child."

"Yes, the child," Sergio responded. "So unfortunate that he escaped. I deeply regret the error. We apologize, señor. My companions were inexperienced with my old boss's talent for deception. I should have warned them about Papá Eli's cane. At the same time, that trick is classic, and they were foolish to take the bait."

"You take the blame and shift it at the same time," said El Dragón. "Do you ever speak with a single tongue? I need to remove it so as not to be disappointed again."

"We know where he is," Izzi interrupted.

"Yes," hastened Sergio, "he's at Eden's Bend, just next door to El Pequeño Jardín. I know the couple who took him in."

"Then why are you meeting me here without the boy and his chaperones?" El Dragón demanded. "Your empty hands are digging your grave."

"Señor," Sergio stuttered, "we are watching Eden's Bend for the right moment, but in these days there is just too much traffic: law enforcement, social workers, ranch hands, construction teams—Señor, the place is as thick as thieves! We'd be caught red-handed if we made a move."

El Dragón pulled on the leash, causing the Komodos to raise their heads toward the two frightened men. "It is better to be red-handed than dead-handed. Hear me: This is the last time I will see you without the child. If I do see you again with empty hands, it will be your last day on earth."

Sergio wiped sweat from his brow. "There is another possibility coming to mind, señor, but a strange one I'll admit. I've not worked out how to do it, but it could be a way to retrieve the child in secret."

Cold silence followed. El Dragón lifted his head. "Go on."

"The child has many friends among the animals at Eden's Bend. He plays with them almost every day. And some are—señor, I kid you not—some are very wild things. They are somehow friends with him. One of them is a spotted panther from the Yucatán. *El tigre.*"

"Explain yourself," said El Dragón with no sign of emotion.

"I mean they are connected—the boy and the jaguar. If you track the one, you will come across the other. If you find the one, you will find the other. If you find them alone, then you have your prize."

El Dragón stood still for so long the only sound was the wind in the branches, which moaned as if stricken by an unseasonal winter. El Dragón opened his mouth, and it seemed as if the temperature dropped even further as he spoke.

"Sergio, I believe you tossed your mind overboard just before you sank the ship. Listen to me: The next time we meet, you will either have the boy and his ill-fated shepherds, or you will become food for my pets. If you think the jaguar can lead you to where the boy is alone and retrievable, then you know what to do. There is nothing else to say. Goodbye."

El Dragón returned to his vehicle. The Komodos looked at Sergio and Izzi until the leash pulled their heads around. The reptiles entered the Impala, climbed over the lap of their owner, and reclined in the seat next to the man. Sitting inside, he did not reflexively check his phone as most do, nor did he say a word to the driver, who had been watching the proceedings with his hand on his weapon. El Dragón brewed upon thoughts that swirled inward like a whirlpool troubled above a boiling fissure on the ocean floor, a fracture that drew all aquatic current and all life into its abyss. Then he drove away.

The other men, after a moment of murmured comments, also drove away.

In the wake of silence the manmachines left behind, the birds froze poised on the oaks, beaks open, wings half outstretched, not knowing whether to hide or fly. Then, one by one, they hopped to a branch above or below, doing so repeatedly, not in rhythm, but each according to their own agitation, such that the foliage appeared to ripple like waters stirred by the passing of a large unseen swimmer beneath the surface or as when a mountain slope swayed by tremors in the heart of the earth yields intermittent streams of soil and stones. So it was as the green jays and the brown jays mourned the unexpected visit of Man.

Gem spoke. "Alas! A wind blows forbidding eggs to hatch! A hailstone cloud comes to destroy the harvest! Man tramples new sprouts and young seedlings, sometimes unawares, sometimes on purpose for fear of what might be. Either way, this rendezvous below us tells me that the time is short. I must depart now in search of Pace and Force!"

And the green jay who had spoken from the center branch beside Gem, returned, lifted up his voice, and sang a song to awaken all to what they now knew they must do:

From the hot breath of Man an ill wind blows
It hushes the jabber and prattle slows
Awakens the feather and stirs up the wing
To flee from the weather instead of to sing

185

For in the storm looming the talk of the bird
Is soon swallowed up by the billowing stir
Ba-boom! Then a crackle of lung-drenching fear
Comes torrenting down onto all who are near

So if there's an airway, a passage of hope
It's not in our chatter or banter or boasts
But helping creation the high ground to find
Until new creation makes all things divine

"Yes!" another green jay agreed. "We will spread the news with you! We greens all will!"

"Our ways are not those of the greens," a younger brown jay said, "for we cannot noise abroad our news even if the brewing wars of Man move us beyond our hunkering."

"True," an older brown jay replied, "but this meeting of Men that just took place tells us that to hunker is only to wait with our backs turned to a high tide that will swallow us alive, just as our green jay cousin just sang. There is no escaping the shortness of the time."

"What should we do then?" the younger asked.

"What else, but to tell others about the lord of the Valley," cried the older one, "both his Council of the Cats and Court of the Animals! Perhaps it is time to lift our beaks again, for a jaguar has come."

"But we are not bold heralds like the greens," another brown jay said.

"That, too, is true," said the older one, "but you know as well as I do, we brown jays can be good gossips of the same message the greens speak openly. We can make a rumor of it, a secret to pass on. Creation loves secrets, and who knows? Our message murmured in the shadows may well fly ahead of the greens' in the sky! As Clifford the Shrewd, our great forefeather in the time of the Wall Street lords, used to say, 'The whispered rumor sprouts its wings while heralds hoarse their voice for kings.' We will therefore keep pace with our cousins. We browns will whisper the rumor while the greens shout it. 'A Council of the Cats and a Court of the Animals will happen soon! The animal kingdom will no longer sleep, for the lord of the Valley has returned!'"

And with that encouragement, Gem and both flocks departed, scattering to spread the news.

The night wind buffeted even more fiercely now, violent enough to provoke crested caracaras to complain from their perches and wild enough to compel the northern pintail ducks to gather for fear of their safety. On Gem flew, announcing her message to the curve-billed thrasher and the groove-billed ani, bobbing and weaving between sabal and cypress.

The wind twisted into a blast of cold, hitting Gem from below and throwing her into a sumac bush. Shaking her head to recover clear thought, she jumped into the air again.

"This wind is not from the gulf!"

"Indeed, it is not," rasped the wind, "for then it would obey the laws of nature. But I am not of this nature. I am its pariah! *Stop*, you senseless messenger! Stop your flying and your calling. Stop spreading vain hope to the birds and the beasts. I have already removed from flight the feathered friends you made at the manplace of the Komodos. All have lost heart. All have dropped their wings. All have fallen silent, the brown as well as the green. The one tribe has returned to hunkering and the other to anxious noise. But you remain, oh foolish and impetuous one, for you were the most deeply deceived. You were taken *in* by beauty, but I will take you *out* by fear! Stop now!"

In the empty space between Gem and a shrub of sweet acacia, the void seemed to become a vertical puddle of dark water. The rippling pool congealed. And as it did, a shape took form, as when plaster for a death mask takes shape over the face of the deceased to reveal the contours after life has departed from it. Thus the dark pool became a visage floating in the air: a face with a misshapen gap for a mouth. A graceless form with lidless eyes mocking in their gaze. A leer and a jeer in the stretch of the cheeks, which seemed in the torpor of rigor mortis as the face grimaced the parody of a smile. The mouth moved.

"Charm has deceived you," the spirit said. "A pit is dug for those who believe in beauty, young green jay. You know it, and I know it too. What is more, from your own mouth you have confessed that there is much you do not know about this jaguar. But I say there is another thing, too, you are ignorant of: You do not know the motive of this spotted beast who has swept your heart away. How do you know he does not intend to devour you once you return to him? For it is written in the fallen stones lining the path of all flesh: 'Beauty is the prelude to betrayal.'"

Gem shivered as she hovered, her wings carrying her body by way of the blast that bent and blew upon her from behind the suspended mask.

"He did not eat me when he saw me!" Gem said with effort.

"Ha!" spat the spirit. "He was full! He had already eaten. He was biding his time, my dear, biding his time till your guard is down. You know, deep down, that nothing good can come of a cat. They are as ruled by their instincts as *you* are. And sooner or later, all the 'good' they espouse is swept away to make room for *greed*. You know this to be true."

"He was good to me when we met," protested Gem. "That is all I know."

The green jay tried to recall her encounter with the jaguar. *Doubt gives my memory a beating like these gusts of wind give my body a beating! How confusing! I can't summon the feelings I knew in the hour of our meeting. Be that as it may, I know without a doubt that I have spoken with the lord of the Valley. And though now all the ethereal colors of that moment fade to monochrome, still, in my heart of hearts, I know I met him.*

Gem opened her beak. For all the whirling wind she still could not easily catch air. She breathed in with straining ribs and spoke in a desperate exhale.

"Your words may be true, but they just as much may be false! At best your words are fifty-fifty! And what do *you* know of this jaguar? You haven't even met him! How can you be so sure about someone you don't even know?"

The spirit laughed scornfully, a derision that drove a family of cactus wrens and a lone chachalaca from their night roosts in hysterical fear; they flew headlong into the night with no sense of direction other than the compelling need to be far from the spirit's wrath. Then the spirit inhaled, and out of his mouth came a lazy river of smooth words, as smooth as the surface of ice warmed by a midday sun, a smoothness giving no clue to the hardening to come at twilight.

"Oh, my dear Gem, my dear, dear Gem. I *do* know him. Indeed, I have known him all his life. He is Oracle of Sian Ka'an, of the manrealm Yucatán. I am old friends with his house—one might say his original friend. I make my home in his kind. He does not own himself. He belongs to me. It has been our tradition since the beginning. We are allies. You cannot believe him, Gem, when he says this Valley is his. That is not the truth. The Valley belongs to me. He is my servant, and he does my bidding. That, my beloved, naive green jay, is the truth!"

Gem shivered uncontrollably. For one thing, it had become unnaturally cold in the pocket of fabricated air confronting her. And for another, the words imparted a chill *inside* her, a shiver of doubt, a dart poison-tipped with the question "What if?" The dart of words deep into the chamber of her thoughts. She tried to open her beak, but it was as if constricting vines hindered her. She shook the smothering off—though it seemed there was no strength left—and opened her mouth in hopes that somehow words would flow against the arctic tide subduing her.

"So…you say he can't be good…and you say he can't be trusted…I'll admit there's not much in this Valley that's good or trustworthy either. I'll grant you that, Cold One, yes, I'll grant you that. But…as I was telling my kin…the brown and the green…I took in a burden that fills me but makes me feel lighter, not heavier.

"I can't say the same for *your* words, Strange One, for—however true they feel—they leave me feeling as if I cannot fly, as if I'll never fly again! That just can't be right. That *can't* be all there is. It's sour fruit I'm tasting, and I want no part of it! 'It's…it's the berries on the tree, not the roots you can't see, that give the branch its name.'"

The spirit hissed and growled as Gem continued.

"So I'm sticking with my task, Confusing One…I'm going to be a stubborn jay, come what may…And besides—*oh* how cold it is! The air stings me to breathe it!—besides all that, I saw a beauty I cannot deny. Even if I've lost the memories of the colors. Even if I've lost the memory of the words. I saw beauty. The quill of my deepest feather bears witness. Not the kind of beauty that charms me, but the kind of beauty that *disarms* me, for in *that* kind of beauty I'm not robbed. I'm not dominated…I'm safe. I'm invited. I can hope again…And who knows but that the beauty I've seen, in the absence of anything good or true, might just go ahead and do the work of *all three*. Now…*get out of my way!*"

And with that, Gem closed her eyes and threw herself beak-first at the frigid image of the spirit. The mask shattered, the air became instantly warm, and all that remained was a distant howling. Whether it was the spirit, the weather, or both, Gem could not tell. Hovering in the air, she panted as she recovered in the space of silence the shattering created.

From beneath the branches of the sweet acacia, a summer tanager emerged. Her bright red feathers appeared dark in the moonlight. She gazed at Gem, who returned her stare with a look of amazement. The green jay brought her wings to rest and alighted upon the bush. Both birds, bonded by the battle they had just witnessed, spoke to one another through the awe on their faces.

"Thank you," sang the tanager in her robin-like way. "I thought winter had come early—but look, instead, a laughter from a future spring! See how the sweet acacia blooms!"

And it had indeed. Even in the dark, the bright yellow blossoms of the sweet acacia sang their presence from a lone branch, the one nearest Gem, radiating a joy that eclipsed the bleak moment a second before.

The tanager gave the green jay hackberries from her cache, and in the strength of that food, Gem hastened on her way.

19

SWOG'S WALLOW

As Gem fought her way through the barrier of the spirit, the two surviving stewards of the Valley were meeting in council, unaware. The ocelot and the bobcat were not friends; they were managers. They stewarded the Valley together, but only on the condition that they meet in a neutral location. They settled on a small island within a muddy depression, which in former times had been the domain of an enormous feral hog named Swog who had ruled that realm with his thick sides for many a year uncontested until one fateful Christmas Eve, when Men from Gaston Ranch had discovered their Christmas Day dinner rolling in the mud.

With the passing of that lumbering legend, what remained was an oval of earth within a moat of ruined ground hinting of its former sludgy state: Swog's Wallow. A thicket of retama, woolly croton, and Cuban jute cloaked an open space in the center of the isle, and this is where Prickleback, the chief of the javelinas, hosted his guests. Because of the Law of Hospitality, the javelina was secure from being eaten by the two carnivores he served. And even if the animals no longer lived by that law with as much sincerity as their ancestors had, the wallow remained safe for Prickleback, for here was one place Force and Pace could agree was a no-hunting zone and neutral ground, if for no other reason than that, for both bobcat and ocelot, it was an equally disagreeable spot for a clean feline.

Pace and Force picked their way through muck to the dry mound in the middle. Licking off the more annoying flecks that would not come loose with a kick, they sat on the patch of grass inside the thicket's ring, where bunchgrass and Bermuda competed for prevalence. But, unlike the blades of grass, which faced each other down at every possible point, the cats did not face each other.

Prickleback reclined near them. His coat, like that of his tribe, was a stiff brindle of brown, gray, and black with a lighter colored ring around neck and shoulders resembling a collar. There was no need to offer his guests a pipe or cigar, for the old wallow created its own peculiar aroma, a mixture of fermenting loam and overripe leaves. The fog had decided to attend the gathering, filling the vacant pond with her airy droplets of water and giving the midnight moon a halo.

The bobcat spoke into the fog. "Salt the owl sent word you wanted to talk to me."

"It is about the House of Canis," said the ocelot, looking into the mist as if the bobcat were on another, unseen island. "One of its clans is riding roughshod over our realm. A young coyote named Thud is rivaling Chief Range for the alpha position of the pack. Thud has broken off with his followers to raid ranches and dens. Also, they cornered a javelina into a mantrap and ate him after it closed on his leg."

At this Prickleback grunted an acknowledgment. "Not fair play! The Code of Parley gives a javelina one chance to charge before he is attacked! But they ate Old Hickory alive while he squealed in the trap! I will never have any dealings with their kind again, except to gouge 'em through!"

Pace looked at Prickleback with lament in his eyes. "They have forgotten the Code, oh Friend of the Prickly Pear. What remains is only 'Kill and eat.'" Then the ocelot turned toward the bobcat. "Force, we have got to do something. Man might blame us cats for the carnage and kill us instead. We need to force this issue to a head with Range. The chief of the coyotes must put his house in order."

"Pah! Foolish!" Force retorted. "Range won't listen to us. He's a coward, like all coyotes. I would rather go after Thud myself than confront Range."

"Then you will just be telling Range that Thud is the alpha male, the very thing Thud wants," replied Pace.

"The very thing *Range* wants is Thud dead," retorted Force. "In doing what I want, I do what Range wants—though that's no matter to me."

"You bet your fur on a fight with Thud's thugs? You're a reckless cat, Force. I shouldn't have expected anything different from your kind. We all know about your sister Roxy's ridiculous feat at the Gladys Porter Zoo, how she snuck in and pounced on a cockatiel right in the middle of a bird show! She almost made off with him before the zookeepers yanked him out of her mouth. She's still the laughingstock of the Valley for that antic."

The bobcat growled. "You dare to raise the name of my *sister* in this council? You have gone too far."

"If only to block *you* from going too far by taking the matter of the coyotes into your own paws. Listen to counsel for once!"

"Who are you to counsel me, Pace? The only thing these coyotes understand is a clamp of the jaw on the throat. I know what to do *without* your words."

The ocelot glowered at the bobcat. "I knew it was useless to consult you!" He lifted his head away from Force as if repulsed by a foul odor. The stripes on Pace's neck arched upward while he looked down at the bobcat. He narrowed his eyes. "You do not understand us ocelots. We are of the *jaguar*. Our spots speak of him. We shadow his territory, and we know how to rule it. We are the House of Pardalis."

The bobcat scowled through his muttonchop beard.

"But there is no jaguar here in the Valley anymore! He's been gone for decades, and without the jaguar, you no longer have anything to 'shadow.' It is *my* territory to rule, for where the cougar does not tread the North Continent, the House of Lynx Rufus rules. Welcome to the realm of the bobcat, Pace."

The ocelot rose, extending his claws as he moved toward the bobcat. "Without the jaguar, *I* am the closest living relative. It is *my* territory; I only consult you as a concession."

"Without the cougar, I am the cat of the north," said Force through his fangs. "It is *my* territory; I only tolerate you because you happen to live here, you and all that's left of your remnant house." He set his shoulders to charge.

Prickleback stood and snorted sharply. "Shut your gobs, you howlers! Have you already forgotten why you came to my mound in the first place? You are here because of Thud, and here is what I say about the trouble he has caused us all: Do not do a thing, I tell you, either of you. Just let the coyotes alone, and they will sort it out themselves. Then the ruckus they make that draws Man into the fray will be on their own heads, and you will have saved your own."

Pace and Force looked at Prickleback as their pupils flared with wounded pride. Their irascible host continued.

"You cannot change their ways, you dreaming felines."

He grumbled as if pushing the words through dirt with his nose. "They can only change if they choose to."

Both cats were panting as the toxin of their anger slowly cooked off in their breath. They ruminated over what the javelina had said. All became quiet. A mourning dove played her melancholy nocturne from somewhere near their misty, mud-bound island. Pace walked a slow circle on the grass, then he sat, looking at the fog-veiled moon. Force stretched his back and rocked his forepaws, his claws poking holes in the sod as he did. He heaved a sigh. The faint hum of an airplane moved through the darkness.

"If only the lord of the Valley were here," Pace bemoaned. "Then the House of Canis would be held accountable when it ravaged, and the ocelots and bobcats would abide by the domains the jaguar would set."

"Yes, if only," groaned Force with the tone of one who has already decided his words are a waste of good air. Nevertheless, the song of the lonesome dove calmed the bobcat, and his wisdom, which, in fits of ill temper, retreated to the tufts of black hair at the tips of his ears, returned to his center. "Your longing is a noble one, my ocelot cousin, and it would cause the restoration of many things in the animal kingdom. But alas, it will never happen. The House of Panthera Onca has been missing in the Valley since the days of our fathers."

"It was the manyear 1946, to be exact," a solemn voice intoned from a retama branch above them. Salt the owl had joined the council at some unknown point during the conversation.

"Hail to you, oh Seer in the Dark," said Force.

"Greetings, oh Sage of Green Island," said Pace. "Welcome to our council in the fog. You know the manyear he disappeared?"

"I do," replied Salt, "and I know the story."

"Why did he vanish?" Force asked.

Salt unfolded and refolded his wings of white and rusty brown, then settled onto his branch. He turned toward the moon, and while she made a gentle pool of light within his eyes, he recalled the reason why.

"The jaguar ruled here long before this mud-bound mound remembers, and for many an age. But when Man, his master, saw him, Man was not content to tame the jaguar only. He coveted his spots—more lovely than the leopard's, I am told—and he craved to drape himself with them.

"And although he bore the honor of being the Maker's prize creation, Man, he was afraid that he was not *truly* Man. That fear drove him. So, to prove it to himself and his neighbor, he slew jaguars right and left, time after time. He thought that by lifting up the great cat's coat from outstretched arm he could declare, 'See, I am Man, for I have killed the lord of the Valley.' And though it is true that the calling of Man is to exercise dominion over us animals, he did not realize that he was truly Man before he killed each jaguar, and he did not rest content that he was truly Man after each one lay slain before him."

The owl stretched out his wings and sang a series of mournful tones in the same note. "Rather than *working with* the glory of the great cat to take each one up at the right time and protect his herds, he devoured the great cat's glory without ceasing for the sake of his own. Thus he craved the spots so much that he kept on killing. And even after cornering Kahoo the Grave, the last jaguar of the Valley, in the manrealm called Old Cavazos—now known as Eden's Bend—Man was still unsure whether he had proven he was master. And so it is to this day. In spite of the many things he dominates, Man never seems to conquer enough to know who he already is."

Salt's account sank into the hearts of his listeners as when the morning flowers sink back into their stems once their bloom is done in the heat of the day. A silence followed. Then Pace lifted his head toward the owl and nodded in courtesy to the counselor in the branches.

"But some seem to know now," Pace commented, "at least regarding us ocelots. Man has made corridors for us to move about, even paths under the great bands of death where his manmachines roar. And I have seen Man take us up, mark us for his own, and set us free again. Some of our kind wear the band of his protection, a 'radio collar' they call it. I have also met ocelots from Tamaulipas who say, 'It was Man who brought us here to strengthen your tribe.'"

"That is true," replied Force, "and that gives some cause for a path other than despair, doesn't it, Salt? Let's hope that Man becomes content with the spots he now drapes himself with and stops his 'craving' as you call it. Until then, we must groan and guard our fur from further harm by whatever means we're gifted with."

20

THE WORD OF THE STEWARDS

Gem reached the thicket concealing Swog's Wallow. Landing on a drought-dry branch of a mesquite, she cocked her head in the opaque air.

"I'm certain there are ocelots and bobcats in here somewhere, most likely the ones I need to see, for I have heard of this meeting place. But the fog doesn't help me find them."

Gem pushed back the murky silence with the alarm-clock call of her kind.

Not far away, Pace and Force listened, still as statues, senses affixed to the sound that came upon their ears from beyond the isle and the moat of muck.

"Are you there?" Gem called into the dark, mixing eagerness and carefulness in equal measure. "I am Gem the green jay. I have news, news that will make your eyes bright."

Pace growled. "A green jay with good news for the stewards of the Valley? Since when do green jays do anything but chide us?"

"I'll say!" scoffed Force. "The only 'news' your tribe has ever brought us is mocking epithets. 'More rivals than rulers!' you chirp beyond reach of our paws.

"I agree with the bobcat!" said Pace. "Your flock flits from branch to branch calling us names. 'More muddlers than managers!' you sing as you flee. And now you change your tune?"

"I change my tune because I myself have changed!" replied Gem. "I carry not only information but transformation!"

Pace guffawed sarcastically. "'Transformation.' We ocelots are trained to be cautious, Miss Green Jay. It is our sacred tradition. It will take more than words in the fog to brighten my eyes."

"And we bobcats are trained to be suspicious," said Force. "It is our solemn oath to be so. For the carcass can be poisoned, and dressed meat a trap, and the open space a shooting range, and the end of your words could point to evil just as much as you claim it points to good."

Salt, observing from a retama branch above, said nothing, but watched with astute focus. Prickleback, too, held his peace, standing tall with the dignity his referee and bouncer roles required.

Gem, now oriented by the voices of the felines, fluttered forward until she came upon Swog's Wallow, squinting in response to the mud-reek below. Then, like a cloud within a cloud, came the pungent scent of the javelina. She turned toward it and also found the scent of the ocelot, a blend of foliage, ponds, and fermenting earth. Then she found the musky odor of the bobcat. She followed the airy trail within the fog-smothered branches until she saw silhouettes sitting beneath her.

Gem alighted on the mound and bowed with one wing across her body and another stretched away, announcing: "The lord of the Valley has returned and requests a Council of the Cats at the place of your choosing."

Pace marveled but immediately furrowed his brow, causing the two-line pattern on the crown of his head to narrow above his eyes.

"How could this be? Kahoo is dead, and we have no word from Mexico. Besides, the border works of Man block the way from the South."

Encouraged by the response, Gem raised her head and hopped a step forward.

"From the *North*, not the South. He has come not from where we expected, but from the North—and from the sky. He lives in the new manrealm called Eden's Bend, toward Laguna Atascosa and the ranches of kings, where animals from near and far roam within fenced boundaries, some three fences deep, some a mere gate away from open country. That is where his paws touched the earth when he arrived from the North and from the sky."

Force growled in annoyance and stepped toward Gem. "From the North and from the sky? Impossible! You mocking jay! Your tribe has a long tradition of precocious talk! Only your cousins the blues are full of more braggadocio, I'm told. What do you want from me—a sliced-open underbelly? Stop your lies!"

Gem hopped back. "But Force, sire, how else could our lord return except through a way that is, as you say, 'impossible'? You affirm that the barrier to Mexico in the South blocks him from coming that way, don't you? So, isn't the North a remaining way he *could* come? And since the *land* of the North is so hostile to the jaguar that it drove his tribe to extinction, why could it not be the *sky* through which he has come? Why is it then unbelievable that he should return from the North and from the sky?"

The logic slowed Force's fuming. "Where did you get such insight, green jay? Your kind is of neither the owls nor the falcons."

"I do not know," Gem chirped, "but the sight of the lord of the Valley seemed to clear up my own, like breaking through a cloud to a deep blue and a long view."

Pace reflected in the pause that followed. He looked at the haloed moon through the fog, and in the periphery of the halo, he saw Salt the owl looking on the council below. Pace opened his eyes as wide as he could and considered the light given him. But Force, being a bobcat, chose investigation over reflection as the best course of action. He hunched forward, his relatively long hind legs lending themselves to the position and giving his gait the appearance that at any moment he might spring upon his prey. He stepped toward the green-winged bird, who felt in herself the potential power of the cat as it touched the slender strength of her bones. She hopped back another wingspan.

The bobcat spoke. "Your words are a wall I cannot scale, I grant you that, but certainly this thing coming *cannot* be a jaguar. It must be some other thing 'from the North and from the sky' as you put it. Yes, I know that the ways by land are too difficult for a great cat of old, but only birds and bats come from the sky, not jaguars. You have heard wrong—or, more likely, you exaggerate." Force leered at Gem. "I suspect your motive."

"Good motive or bad, you cannot judge," Gem mused, relieved that Force had chosen a conversation over a carnivorous ending. "Only I know what my motive is, for only I am in my heart, not you—I did not come here to argue with you, Force, but to *help* you, and to help you too, Pace. The jaguar has returned to the Rio Grande Valley, and if you don't believe green jays like me, ask the great kiskadee. Go and ask the cattle egret, who, as you know, seldom speaks, preoccupied as he is with picking ticks off smelly hides. Ask the tribes of the small folk, too, for the news travels through the burrows as fast as it does the branches."

Force listened, and, as he considered, Pace lowered his gaze from the moon and pondered aloud. "Kiskadees don't lie, and small folk have no interest in a big story, for they are only small things, safe from the rivalries of the large and the strong."

Force turned to his fellow steward. "That is true, oh Ocelot Prince. You and I are dignified felines too visible to avoid a big story, but the small folk are free of such a burden. I daresay I envy them, for they have quietly found a way to live in the cleared land of the manplaces. Their goal is not to reform the animal kingdom, but to adapt to the present dismal circumstances."

Pace nodded in agreement. "And adapt they have, my Lynx Rufus rival. Therefore, there is no good reason for them to proclaim a return of someone who has not actually returned."

The bobcat smirked. "In fact, if anything, the return of the jaguar would upset the safe world the small folk have made for themselves. It may return things to the wild, and this would mean other things would return as well, like bravery and pain and perseverance—things which would make the small folk very uncomfortable...But what are we doing talking like this! Listen to how we sound! Philosophizing while sitting still will get us nowhere. Before we know it, we'll be making jaguars out of shapes in the fog!"

And the bobcat's wisdom retreated from his center as he chastised himself for hoping.

Pace stepped toward the green jay. "This word you give is new, Gem, too new to pounce on without a ponder and a pause. If it is true, it will change everything for both the great and the small." He retuned his gaze to the moon and spoke, so that it was unclear whether the ocelot was speaking to the one above him or the one beside him.

"Maybe it *is* true, in which case our pause should be for planning, not entertaining doubts."

Force stared hard at Pace until the power of his glare pulled the ocelot back down to earth. "Why are you so eager for this news to be true?"

Paced glared back. "I am not trying to make something true that is not. You speak as if my wishes for a jaguar would somehow have the power to conjure him! No, I am only certain about this one thing: If it is accurate the lord of the Valley is on his way, we had better respond to his arrival. We must gather the cats, and we must send scouts to listen to the coyotes, that we might ascertain in their incessant yippings and yappings whether they know this rumor too. We are the ones who have been in charge in the jaguar's absence, and if it is true he has come, he will ask us for an account. We must receive our ruler."

Salt hooted a series of fluid, one-note sounds. "The time for saying 'if it is true' has passed, for it is true indeed. I have seen the jaguar with my own eyes. The lord of the Valley has returned after a sabbath of seventy springs."

"What?" Force exclaimed. "You have seen him! Then why didn't you tell us before?"

"It would not have honored the messenger to usurp her message," Salt answered, "and it would not have honored you to forestall your wrestling therewith, for struggle is where the best roots grow. It is the same as when a tree presses through the rocky crag of a canyon side. Once it has done so, both root and rock together make the tree more fixed than any sap-rich seedling in shallow soil, where flash floods and feverish summers extinguish the poorly rooted life. You will need deep roots for what lies ahead, oh Stewards of the Valley.

"And besides all that, High-Minded Ones, it was better to save my news until your debates had strutted about and collapsed on the grass. Then you are willing to listen. Such is the way of the House of Glaucidium. As our renowned ancestor Gleamengel used to say, 'Exhausted legs lead to open ears.' Now you are ready to counsel one another about where your feline gathering should take place."

Prickleback snarled and coughed as if, while foraging, his tongue had encountered a bitterweed herb. He shook off his role of host and raised his snout.

"What kind of 'counsel' is this! I have never heard of such a thing. Jaguar indeed! Has everyone here but me lost his bristle? This cannot be true! And even if it *were* true—I am as mindless as a water bug to speak such an idea—what reason would my kind have for being happy about it? Are we not a savory meal for this predator? Are we not a delicacy to his maw?

"Therefore, *No*, I say, an absolute *No*: I do not accept the news of the coming of this cat. If it is not true, then I remain the only animal on this mound with eyes in his head. And if it *is* true, then I remain committed to opposing him. Why, I would even help the coyotes and the cottonmouth drive him out! Yes, I know that those two bite my kind also, Old Hickory not the least of my noble line who has perished before their fangs. But as Jorge the Just, that ruler of our tribe in the days of Santa Anna used to say, 'Better the devil you know than the devil you don't.' One way or another, I shall resist this jaguar to the last fang in my snout and the last of my fourteen toes!"

Prickleback's rant attracted his dozing herd, led by Sweat, his master sergeant. They gathered behind their speechmaking chief. Prickleback was startled by the sudden assembly of his followers.

I find myself in such a flow of captivating rhetoric that it seems indecorous to discontinue, even if to continue is to go an

*acorn's throw beyond what I really think once the fumes of my
wrath are dissipated. But here before me is my tribe, and here I
am, their brave leader. My words must flow on.*

He cleared his throat and chopped his jaws, making a
popping sound with his teeth.

"Hear ye, oh herd renowned for its reclusive prowess and
peace-loving ways. We are cornered again—I weary to say
it—cornered again by the invasion of a tribe. We know all too
well the invasion of the feral hogs, those piggish gluttons who
ruin our rivers and trample the acorn before it can become
so much as a two-leaf sprout. Bullying their way through our
forests with their ever-growing brood, they waylay the works
of Man, who mistakes us for them all too often and slays us
in their stead! While their squealing hordes devour the best
of the land, we must hide in the thornscrub, grateful for the
grace the spines give but pierced by the truth that *we*, yes, *we*
are the rightful heirs of this soil and its bounty—but cannot
enjoy it!"

"Hear, hear!" shouted Sweat as the herd raised their snouts
in squeals of affirmation. They did not notice the dismay in
the eyes of Prickleback as he foraged for more rhetoric in the
storeroom of his mind. He found more.

"And what is worst of all, worse than this usurpation of
our domain, is that the Namer has of late misnamed us. He
has given us another name, so the laughing chachalacas tell
me. It has reached my ears that Man not only calls us *las javelinas* as the Tejanos of the old frontier did, feeling the point
of our spear-like teeth in their legs when they threatened our
little ones. No, not only by that noble name does Man call us.
Recently, some of them have named us *javelina hogs*, as if *we*
were of that mud-caked tribe and conspirators in their crimes.
Do they not know that we are of the House of Pecari Tajacu
while they are of the wretched House of Sus Scrofa? Why,

all the creatures of the Valley know, and the Maker besides, that *there is no such thing as a javelina hog.* Man, with his weak eyes, has confused honeysuckle with guinea grass—and branded them both as unwanted weeds!"

The javelinas, incensed at the slander, squealed protests and woofed curses.

What else can I do but continue? Prickleback concluded as he saw his tribe's response. *What else can a fallen pine cone do but roll down the hillside it finds itself on?* He took a deep breath.

"And now, oh peace-loving peccaries, listen to me. Your self-protection is the stuff of legends from the days of the First Nations to the invading armies of north and south who stalked us for our tasty flesh before the European hogs overran us. Let us not wait to be overrun again. Let us not be as gullible as Man's dairy cows, who don't know the difference between the milking parlor and the butchery, ambling with equal naivete into both. If it be true the jaguar has indeed returned, not only should we evade him, let us *resist* him. For you see all too well what woes our hospitality to the hogs brought upon us: We offered a hoof, and they took the whole shank! Oppose this lord of the Valley for your sake and the sake of your families!"

"Enough, host," interrupted Salt from above. "Your words will get you in trouble with the jaguar. You are cornered already, and you had best make terms with him."

Prickleback looked up and murmured an earthy noise of irritation at the owl's words. (He could not see him in the tree, being myopic, as all javelinas are.)

"Yes," Force conceded, "now that Salt has confirmed Gem's message, we are cornered and cannot keep our old ways. This thing the green jay and the owl speak of is new."

Prickleback scoffed. "Whether I am cornered or not makes no difference to me. A javelina is a javelina: mulish in preference. What he wants, he holds on to. Some call it stubbornness, but we call it strength."

Prickleback trotted off the mound into the dark. His herd followed. Together they crossed the mudflats, the thick goo thereof squishing through the space between their cloven hooves, such that their movement through the mud was a refrain of one kick-away of clod for every two steps forward. They came to the mouth of a branchy corridor and followed it to a place among the mesquite where Prickleback rallied his herd with a stirring speech on the hallowed tradition of stubbornness in the House of Pecari Tajacu. The sound of their squeals and snortings lingered in the ears of the cats for a moment, then faded away as the herd moved on. And as it faded, Force and Pace agreed to call a Council of the Cats.

"But only on the condition we hold the council at Salazar's Wood," insisted Force, "for I own the hunting grounds there, and a deep, defendable den. If there is treachery afoot, my tribe shall be ready. And we will grant the ocelots passage if escape be our only trail before the cat of the House of Panthera Onca."

"I do not anticipate treachery from our ruling cousin," said Pace, "but from some other quarter, yes, betrayal is always hiding in the brush. And because of that hidden threat, I agree with the location. For my tribe is less than a hundred strong, and for us to gather in one place is to risk the wiping out of our whole line, should some cunning act overtake us. Yes, then, let us meet at Salazar's Wood."

The ocelot arose, the elongated patterns of his coat fluidly unfolding. He joined the tawny bobcat, whose spots resembled a flock of escaping shadows. Together, they faced the green-feathered emissary while the sharp-eyed sage above them watched.

"Gem," Force commanded, "come closer."

The green jay steeled her courage before the carnivores and crossed the cheerless grass that lay between her and them. She lifted her head and looked into the faces of the stewards of the Valley. A faint glow filled the lantern-like eyes of the cats, revealing a hunger for something deeper than food.

"Dispatch the decree," Pace said. "A Council of the Cats at Salazar's Wood whenever the way opens for the lord of the Valley to find that trail. Tell the jaguar we give our word it shall be so. And tell him this word too… 'Welcome.'"

THE PATH IN THE DARKNESS
BOOK 4 OF THE JAGUAR ORACLE SERIES

Receive advance notice of the release of *The Path in the Darkness*, along with Kurt's **free discovery tool, "Recollect Watermark Moments,"** a reflective exercise to help you begin again after a success, a setback, or the start of a new life season. Click the link or scan the QR code here.

http://eepurl.com/hluwu1

"The story reminds me of why I fell in love with Narnia so long ago."
—Amazon Reviewer

Post a Book 3 Review

If you enjoyed *The Search for the Shadow Cat*, please consider leaving a review on Amazon. Your feedback helps other readers find this story!

ABOUT THE AUTHOR

Kurt helps those who built someone else's dream finally build their own.

As a speaker, advisor, and award-winning poet, he draws from twenty years of lived experience in forty nations.

He is a sought-after voice on five continents, advising expats in places as challenging as Cuba, Persia, and North Korea. He has published multiple books, hundreds of articles, and well-respected poetry.

Kurt and his wife Karen have been married since 1993 and raised their family in Afghanistan, where they founded a community development agency. They are Americans living in the Emirates with ties to the Gulf Coast, the Rio Grande Valley, Central Texas, Louisiana, and New England.

He writes in the poetic tradition, inspired by the wonder of creation, the mysteries of the Ancient Faith, and the drama of the nations. Guiding sources for his work include the

Hebrew prophets, the Desert Fathers, Dante, Milton, George MacDonald, C.S. Lewis, and Tolkien.

Why? Because thought leaders go back to the beginning to find the way forward.

The key to the future begins with a memory. Our calling comes from the original self the Creator had in mind when He said, "Let there be you."

To initiate your own return to what matters most, **receive Kurt's free discovery tool,** *Recollect Watermark Moments*—a reflective guide to help you begin again after a success, a setback, or the stirrings of a new season—subscribe at kurtmahler.com, where you will find his writings on the Ancient Faith, original poetry, and a portal to invite him as a keynote speaker.

For those ready to invest in the deep work of personal transformation, Kurt accepts a small number of coaching clients at a time—leaders and creators prepared to ask themselves, **"What one brave thing will I do today?"**